MURDER FOR LOVE

Molly Sutton Mysteries 4

NELL GODDIN

Beignet Books

This book was originally published as *Red for Love*.

For my ever-skeptical and magnificent children, Julian and Nellie.

CONTENTS

J uly 2006

MOLLY WOKE UP FIRST, thanks to Bobo's wet nose in her ear. The morning was warm and she had been sleeping without any covers, so it was easy enough to slip out of bed without waking Ben.

"Come, Bobo," she whispered, to keep the speckled dog from leaping on the bed. Molly went straight for the coffee press and put the water on while Bobo danced around the kitchen hoping for something delicious to fall from the sky.

All things considered, it had been a blissful few months in Castillac. Order had been restored after the Valerie Boutillier abduction, and the village was its usual lively summer self, with *fêtes* and informal get-togethers and everyone in a generally sunny mood. Bookings at La Baraque were excellent.

And of course...there was Ben.

Molly had arrived in Castillac in part to recover from a

divorce. It hadn't been a dragged-out, mud-slinging, litigious kind of divorce, but still, it had been painful to have her dream of a cozy family shattered. Molly thought that a change of scenery— all the way from the suburbs of Boston to Castillac, France— would help her get over it. And it had, with the help of new friends and a *lot* of pastry.

She had most certainly not been looking for romance. She was nearly forty, after all, and already on the road to making peace with the fact that her love life (not to mention childbearing years) might well be behind her. Ben Dufort was a bit younger and the attractive former chief gendarme of the village. He had hardly swept her off her feet; instead, their friendship had deepened slowly, over time, almost without their realizing it. And now that they were together, with everyone in the village knowing about it —and mostly approving, villagers judging these matters freely— Molly was happier than she could remember being in a long, long time.

Just as she was pouring her first cup, she heard a quick rapping on the front door that she recognized as Constance, who helped clean the gîtes on Changeover Day. Quickly Molly slurped some coffee and drank it down, then again. It was wise to have a bit of fortification before facing Constance first thing in the morning.

"Molls!" Constance exclaimed, moving quickly into the foyer when Molly opened the front door. Her shoulder-length hair was pulled back into a ponytail, the hairstyle she wore when she was ready to get to work.

"Bonjour, Constance," said Molly, drinking more coffee.

"Thérèse is out! *Gone!* Just like that!"

Molly blinked. "What are you talking about? Gone where?"

"Our gendarme, Thérèse Perrault!" said Constance impatiently. "Come on, Molly, wake up! I heard she got notice of a new posting but didn't tell anyone. Didn't want a fuss, I guess, though why anyone would pass up a going-away party is beyond me!"

"Are you saying she's left the village already?"

"Yes, Molls, that's exactly what I'm saying! Wake up, little cabbage!"

Molly frowned. Thérèse had said she wouldn't be able to stay in Castillac much longer—the gendarmerie liked to move its officers around, in an attempt to keep them objective—but she hadn't said a word about the move being imminent. Molly would sorely miss her. For one thing, Thérèse had respect for Molly's sleuthing abilities and wasn't shy about slipping her information in order to get Molly's help on difficult cases. It was Thérèse who had told Molly about the note taped to the gendarmerie door saying that someone had seen Valerie Boutillier.

"Want some coffee?" she asked, a troubled expression on her still-sleepy face.

"No thanks. Any chance your guests have cleared out yet? I'd like to get going and finish cleaning early. Thomas wants to take me somewhere for a picnic," she added, grinning.

"It's not even nine, Constance."

"Can't we do something to pry them out of there?"

Molly laughed. "No, you goose. I want their last moments at La Baraque to be happy ones, so that they leave leave feeling wistful and want to come back! Not cursing the cleaner who was knocking on their bedroom window and playing loud music, or whatever it is you have in mind. And speaking of happy moments, I should zip into the village and get some pastry for their last breakfast. You have any other tidbits of news for me? Everything staying relatively harmonious in the village?"

Constance held her chin and looked up at the ceiling, thinking it over. "Yep! No divorces, no burglaries, and no dead bodies. Castillac is an ocean of calm!"

"It's early yet," said Molly, under her breath. Not because she was hoping for mayhem, but because she was learning that no place stayed free of it for long.

A SATURDAY NIGHT in July was more or less perfection in Castillac, thought Molly, for once taking a little care in how she dressed. The weather was exquisitely comfortable, the village blanketed in flowers, and the mood of the villagers buoyant. People were casting around for something to celebrate. One of Therese's friends had decided to have a going-away party for her at Chez Papa even though the guest of honor had already left town, and the idea was so silly that almost everyone Molly knew was planning to go.

"I remember that little black dress you wore to the I'Institut Degas gala," said Ben, who was lying on the bed reading the news on his tablet and glancing at Molly as she got ready.

"I remember dancing the Hustle with you," laughed Molly, and came over to ruffle her hand through his brush-cut hair and give him a quick kiss. "So you're coming tonight? Our being together is old news now, so people won't tease us anymore, right?"

"Stop teasing? Never," said Dufort, rolling his eyes. "Yes, of course I'm coming. No better place to find out what's on people's minds."

"So...you think of yourself as on duty, in a way? Even though you're a detective without a case?"

"Without a case *or* a job. But no, I don't mean it that way, exactly—it's not like I'm coldly trying to sniff out information or anything like that. I'm just used to keeping an eye on things is all. And people do seem to tell me their problems."

"Castillac needs a psychiatrist, maybe that can be your next career!"

"Ha. I'm just hoping you're going to wear that black dress again...."

"It's too hot for that," said Molly, blushing. "And come on, get ready—we should be leaving by now."

Molly was standing next to the bed and Ben reached for her hand and pulled her over. "I don't feel like sharing you at the moment," he said softly, kissing her on the neck. And Molly thought again, closing her eyes, that she could not believe her luck. Like so many women, she could fall into the trap of seeing only the ways she did not match up to supermodels in magazines —her legs were short and she was hardly reed-thin—and it was a delight to see herself if only for moment through Ben's appreciative eyes.

She had never dreamed, back when she was selling off her furniture and saying goodbye to the house in the Boston suburbs where her marriage had ended, that she would ever feel this light again.

Moving to Castillac was turning out to be the best thing she had ever done.

❧

AN HOUR later Molly and Ben drove their scooters down rue des Chênes to Chez Papa. People were spilling out of the bar, standing on the sidewalk, laughing and drinking. A couple of dogs were underfoot. Alphonse had strung multi-colored blinking lights in the scraggly tree nearby and the villagers' faces kept changing colors.

"*Salut!*" shouted Nico from behind the bar as they made their way inside. Frances was perched on a stool at the end of the bar, her black hair freshly cut in a Louise Brooks bob, her lipstick an arresting red. Molly put her arm around her old friend and they kissed cheeks. Ben wandered off to talk to a group in the corner, people Molly had met but didn't know well.

"So how's everything?" asked Frances, lighting a cigarette.

"You're smoking again?"

Frances shrugged "No. In fact, anything you see that suggests such a thing is an illusion, a trick of the eye, simply—"

"Your sarcasm—"

"Oh, Molly, don't you ever feel like just kicking up your heels and doing all the bad things for once? Not caring about tomorrow but just living for the moment as deeply and pleasurably as you can?"

Molly considered.

"*Bonsoir*, Molly dear," said Lawrence Weebly, appearing out the crowd. He was holding his usual bright red Negroni and dressed in a beautiful suit, probably vintage.

"Frances is suggesting we throw all caution to the winds and live for the moment," said Molly. "I'm thinking it over."

Lawrence shrugged. "I lived for the moment for quite some time, when I was young," he said. "I have to say it was overrated."

"What a bunch of fuddy-duddies," said Frances, taking a long drag on her Galois. "Okay, I won't offer either of you a cig, though I bet deep down you're desperate to be cool like me. Smoking's not the only way to live for the moment. What about romance? Or throwing your life up in the air and doing something completely new and different?"

"Done and done," said Molly, "If we'd had this conversation back in Boston, before my marriage broke up and I quit my job and moved here? Then I'd be with you all the way." She shrugged. "But I'm...I'm really happy now. Content, even. Not looking to shake anything up. What about you, Franny? I would have said you already live for the moment pretty well. It's not like you let the usual conventions put a damper on, well, anything you get it in your head to do. Doesn't your family think you're practically a monster?"

Frances laughed. "Oh, of course, but honestly, they don't count. My family thinks if you wear linen in the wrong month you should be separated from polite society, perhaps permanently."

"Her family is koo-koo," Molly said to Nico, who grinned, then looked past Molly as more people were coming up to the bar.

"Au revoir, Thérèse!" someone outside shouted, lifting a glass.

Molly noticed that Nico was smiling broadly at someone behind her, and she turned to see whom he was looking at. A foot away stood a stunning woman, smiling back at Nico. She had long dark hair that tumbled past her shoulders in loose waves, and lovely—*really* lovely—features. But the most arresting thing about her was her eyes, which were tipped up on the outer corners, heavily made-up, and a mesmerizing color of blue-green. Molly realized she was staring but did not want to look away.

"Everything well with you, Iris?" Nico was saying to the woman.

Iris nodded and smiled, but Molly did not believe her. She did not know this woman, had never even seen her before, but she knew a fake smile when she saw one.

Molly gave Nico the "introduce me" stare, but Nico did not get the message.

"So how's everything in Benny-Land?" Frances asked Molly.

"Must you talk to me like we're still in sixth grade?"

"Aren't we?" cackled Frances, taking a sip of her drink followed by a long pull on her cigarette. "I'll tell you, I've been absolutely swamped with deadline after deadline for the last three months. I've hardly been outside, I've done nothing but work. So I'm proclaiming that from here on, this will be the Summer of Fun. Starting....*now!*"

Molly turned away from Frances and saw that Nico had not heard his girlfriend rambling on, and that he was still looking dreamily into the eyes of the woman behind her, chatting as he slowly made her drink. He was going to be useless for an introduction, so Molly clumsily took matters into her own hands, moving back suddenly from the bar and nearly bumping into her.

"So sorry!" said Molly, turning to her.

"No problem," said Iris.

Again Molly had the sensation of wanting to do nothing but look into Iris's eyes and stare at her beautiful face. Her hair was streaked with gray but instead of making her look old, she looked wonderfully exotic, even wise. "Are you a friend of Therese's?" Molly asked.

The woman looked confused. "Thérèse?"

"Thérèse Perrault, the gendarme? This is her going-away party. Even though she's already gone." Molly smiled. "Any excuse to celebrate, I guess, huh? My name's Molly Sutton. I'm American, but moved to Castillac almost a year ago."

"Hello, Molly Sutton," said Iris politely. "Your French is not half bad." She paused and thought for a moment. "I did know Thérèse, years ago, when she was a child. I cook for the school, at the *cantine*, so I end up getting to know almost everyone in Castillac that way. Let's see," she said, looking up at the ceiling, "I believe Thérèse was very fond of *pâté* and did not like mushrooms."

"Heathen," said Molly, and Iris laughed, though her beautiful blue-green eyes seemed sad.

"Iris! I told you I have to get up at dawn tomorrow, I'm starting the staircase at the Lafont's. Why did you order another drink? We need to leave now."

"*Bonsoir*, Pierre," Molly said, loud enough to be heard over the din.

"Oh, *salut*, Molly," said Pierre Gault, his expression not softening much. "I see you've met my wife," he added.

"I've been meaning to call you, actually," said Molly. "Would you swing by *La Baraque* when you have a moment? There's a crumbling barn I want to show you, see what you think. Your husband did some very good work at my place, rebuilding a pigeonnier. Guests love what you did with it," she said, looking back and forth from Iris to Pierre.

"I've got a big job now at the Lafont's, building an extension to their house. Don't know when I'll have time for anything else, but I'll come have a look."

"Thanks!" said Molly brightly.

"Out!" said Pierre under his breath to Iris, and she took a sip of her drink and nodded to Molly before following him through the crowd and into the summer night.

❧ 2 ❧

J uly 7, only two more days of school. The children were wild
with excitement and the heady anticipation of freedom,
and the staff wearily looked forward to the summer break
as well. Caroline Dubois, who worked in the office, was
using her lunchtime to try to bring order to the principal's desk,
as futile a task as that was.

"Tristan," she said quietly to her boss, "if you would just sort
the email as you receive it, it would not pile up in such an
ugly mess."

"I don't mind mess," said Tristan Séverin cheerfully. "Which I
suppose is a lucky thing, considering."

"I suppose so," agreed Caroline, shaking her head. She was a
pretty young woman, dressed in tailored clothes that flattered her
figure. "I understand if you don't want to give me a play-by-play,
but you did mention last month that you were trying something
new for your...your trouble with focusing? Has it helped at all?"

She asked the question but was fairly sure she knew the
answer, since Séverin's desk was as messy as ever, and he still
needed constant reminders of his schedule to keep from missing
meetings. He was a very successful school administrator, beloved

by many families in Castillac for his generosity and creativity in helping their children. But organized and focused he was not.

"Fish oil," scoffed Tristan. "I would much rather just eat more fish, you know? But the doctor insists I take the supplement. Can't tell any difference at all, except that occasionally I have the most unpleasant burps." Tristan grinned.

"More than I wanted to know," said Caroline, gathering up a heap of files from a corner of his desk. "Well, your breath might be bad but I suppose you do have your charms," she added, shaking her head and smiling.

"I'm glad you feel that way," said Tristan. "I don't know what I would do without you," he said, waving a hand at his desk, from which papers were spilling onto the floor on one side and which held a number of empty coffee mugs. "Now let's talk about the rest of the day, and then I'm going over to the *cantine* to have a last lunch with the children. This afternoon I'm meeting with those parents from Salliac, correct? And then the district video-call after that?"

Caroline nodded and sorted the files at the same time. "That's right. Maybe that fish oil *is* doing something for you," she said with a chuckle. Tristan beamed at her and took off, his shirt untucked in back and a flurry of papers falling off the desk as he went by.

The remainder of the school day passed without incident and Caroline got to leave a few minutes early. She would still be coming to work, school or no school; her vacation wasn't until August. But nonetheless it felt like an achievement, getting through another school year, and even though there were still two more days left, she looked forward to getting home and making an effort to celebrate, however underwhelmingly: a kir royale, enjoyed by herself out in her small yard, with her dog and cat for company.

❧

"IF I WERE YOU, I'd just paint right over it," said Molly's old friend Frances, who had come to Castillac for a visit and never left. She was lying back on the old sleigh-bed, watching Molly work.

"I considered that. But see all these seams in the wallpaper? That's going to look terrible painted over, unless I use some technique other than simply one color with a roller, and I don't have the patience to learn anything new right now."

"Don't you think this wallpaper has some vintage charm? It's faded in a pleasant, old-fashioned way." Frances got up on her knees and ran her hand over the wall behind the bed. "Have any of your guests complained?"

"I've only had one guest stay here—Wesley Addison. He wasn't...interior decorating was not one of his subjects. Blessedly. Now call me superstitious...but something about this room gives me the creeps. I call it the Haunted Room, though obviously not to the guests. I'm thinking that a little refreshing of the decor might help lift the creepy factor, you know?"

"Let me see," said Frances, lying on her back and closing her eyes. "I'm communing with the spirits...remember when we used to do Ouija Board?"

"You mean when you would shove that thing around and try to scare me?"

"Yeah," laughed Frances. "Man, I miss being a kid. Just thinking about those days makes me miss the Julys of childhood, because they lasted forever."

"And your mom made really good lemonade."

"Only homemade will do!" said Frances, imitating her mother's voice.

Molly laughed. Then she took the scorer she'd found at the hardware store and scraped it over the wallpaper. Then dipped a sponge in a bucket of water and wiped it over the wall.

"Is that really going to loosen the glue?" asked Frances.

"Youtube says so. And youtube is never wrong."

"Ha."

"So how are things with Nico going? Give me an update."

"Well...."

Molly glanced over her shoulder at her friend, who was grace-fully raising her arms and legs to imaginary music, as though dancing ballet while lying in bed. "I don't know, Molls. Love is...tricky."

"Indeed," said Molly. She put down the sponge and scraped tentatively at the soggy wallpaper with a putty knife, then put some force into it, making heaps of the stuff go splat onto the old sheet she'd spread on the floor. "Boy oh boy, this is satisfying. Goodbye sinister faded roses that remind me of a horror movie!"

"I thought you were obsessed with roses."

"I sort of am. But if you knew the movie I'm talking about, you'd be over here helping me get rid of the wallpaper as fast as possible, believe me."

Frances made no move to get up. "Who's staying in your *gîtes* now? I don't think I've met them. Anybody I'd like?"

"I can't really say. An artist is staying in the *pigeonnier* by himself—Roger Finsterman. He's usually out early in the morning, sitting in the meadow with a sketchpad, although once when I peeked at his sketch it was a wild abstract drawing, nothing to do with the meadow at all that I could see. There's an American couple in the cottage. I've barely seen them, though they've only been here a few days. They have a car and leave early in the morning and don't come back until after dinner."

"I think you should have a party every week for everybody. Nothing fancy, just like...an *apéro* so the guests can be introduced to each other."

"Great idea," said Molly, "but maybe I'll wait until I have a few more *gîtes* up and running. A party with 3 guests is a little hard to get moving, don't you think? Or are you offering to come over every week and provide some entertainment?"

"I can dance," said Frances, saying 'dance' in a terrible French accent. "Or maybe, given your not-so-secret love of detective work, you could put on one of those mystery evenings, where everyone dresses up and plays a part, and tries to figure out who the murderer is."

"Always wanted to do that. But I've had my fill of detecting lately. Right now I want nothing more than to just work on *La Baraque*, hang out with you and Ben, and enjoy the simple pleasures of a Castillac summer."

"Yeah, right," said Frances, smiling to herself as she went downstairs in search of lemonade.

❧ 3 ❧

On Tuesday the rain came down in buckets and the sky was gray and forbidding. Molly spent the first few hours of the day scraping off the remainder of the wallpaper in the Haunted Room, and then, no surprise to anyone who knew her, she had a powerful hankering for an almond croissant. On the scooter it was just a quick trip to *Pâtisserie* Bujold—the best pâtisserie in the département—but did she want to risk getting drenched? The rain had mostly stopped for the moment but the skies had that not-quite-done look.

"What do you think, Bobo?" she asked the speckled dog, who was hovering under her feet as she stood in the front doorway. "I know you don't like being rained on but I don't really mind. Or maybe I'm just saying that because...there's an *almond croissant* at the end of the rainbow. Wouldn't you run through the rain for a big juicy bone? Yeah, I thought so." She squatted down and gave the dog a long scratch behind the ears. Bobo flopped on her back and presented her belly, and Molly gave it a rub, trying and failing to get pastry off her mind.

So leaving Bobo safe and dry, Molly put on a slicker and hopped on her dented brown scooter, which looked a little better since the rain had washed most of the dust off, and zipped straight to Pâtisserie Bujold, the best pastry shop in the village, or even the entire Dordogne, her mouth watering all the way.

Not surprisingly, the shop was empty and Molly had the proprietor's full attention. "Bonjour Monsieur Nugent," she said, folding her arms over her chest without thinking about it.

"Bonjour, Madame Sutton," Edmond Nugent answered, grinning broadly and giving her his usual avid once-over. He was not a tall man, with short arms and legs and a small round belly. That day he sported the beginnings of a moustache, coming in nicely.

Molly walked the length of the two cases, looking at all the kinds of pastry available that day. Sure, she had come in thinking definitely almond croissant, but now that she was there, she felt compelled to check out everything and then decide anew.

Then she was struck with an idea. "Monsieur Nugent, I'm wondering—just how difficult is it to make an almond croissant? It's just puff pastry and almond paste, right? Not too many ingredients?"

Monsieur Nugent looked down at his feet and shook his head, "Oh, my dear Madame Sutton. Are you getting silly ideas in your head? Thinking that you might be able to do what it has taken Monsieur Nugent many, many years to learn?" He lifted his head then and looked into her eyes with such emotion Molly took a step back.

"Well, of course I would never dream that I could do it as well as you. Do you have a lot of helpers? I only ever see you here in the shop."

"I...I hire, from time to time." Nervously he paced back and forth behind the cases. "The fact is that my standards are extremely high, as I have always, from the first time you came in the shop, believed you comprehended and appreciated. I trust I have shown you—" Nugent waved a hand at a framed award on the wall behind him, the paper turning brown around the edges.

"My pastry is *award-winning*," he said. "Not just any old thing tossed out of an oven without care."

"I don't mean to cause offense!" Molly jumped in. "Of course your pastries are the best. The *best!* I tell all my guests not to even think of shopping anywhere else." She paused, letting her gaze linger on an apricot tart, each rounded fruit glossy with glaze and vividly orange, not a crumb out of place. "But I just thought...if I were able to pull off even a much less accomplished version than yours, then on a day like this—" the rain thundered down on the roof of the shop and passersby hurried along the sidewalk, umbrellas angled into the wind— "I could just whip up a little something at home, you understand? Just to get by. Sort of like having extra candles for when the electricity goes out."

Monsieur Nugent understood only too well. Every so often a wave of do-it-yourselfism swept through the village, and while his business was solid and never threatened as a result, still, it ate at Monsieur Nugent to lose customers, even if only for a week or so. He felt that he had earned the right to be the sole purveyor of almond croissants to Molly Sutton—earned it by his hard work, diligence, and artful talent—and was not disposed to look kindly on anything that might take that away.

He had read of the low-carb craze in America that left local bakeries in ruins, and he shuddered at the thought. And for the non-dieters, one could buy ready-made puff pastry at the supermarket. Undoubtably it was of loathsome quality, but Nugent suspected that do-it-yourselfers might be willing to make sacrifices for the satisfaction of independence. Fools and idiots, he thought darkly, not doing much of a job of hiding his displeasure from Molly.

"On occasion I have banned customers from my store," he said in a low voice.

Molly took another step back. "What? Are you *threatening* me, Monsieur Nugent?" Molly had to suppress a *giggle*. It's not that she didn't take pastry seriously—hell, it was a mainstay of her new life—but seriously, he would *ban* her for wanting to cook something herself every once in a while?

Nugent put his hands on the counter and gripped tightly. He had been up since three in the morning, feeling extra stressed since the humid weather made for certain complications with dough. Of all the things he could have imagined happening that rainy day, losing one of his best customers was on the list.

"I have a better idea," he said, forcing his tone to sound gentler. "It is not the lost business that concerns me, Madame Sutton. It is that you, a lovely woman who truly appreciates my art, should be reduced to eating the scraps and mistakes that are the inevitable result of trying to learn something so complex. What I suggest is this: that you allow me to give you lessons in pastry-making. That way, you will at least start off on the right foot."

Molly's eyes widened. Pastry lessons from a master would undoubtedly be an amazing experience. On the other hand, spending hours alone with Monsieur Nugent in a kitchen—without a counter between them—no. She quickly imagined the process would turn into slapstick, with Monsieur Nugent chasing her around the pastry table and reaching for her with his floury hands. It would never work.

"You are so kind, Monsieur Nugent, but really, it was just a moment's whim. Would you give me six almond croissants and that delectable apricot tart? I think I will surprise some of my guests with dessert on the terrace this evening, if the weather clears up."

Monsieur Nugent looked crestfallen. "As you wish," he said, the light in his expression going dim. He put her pastries in a bag and the tart in a box, took her money, and said nothing further.

THAT EVENING the rain finally petered out, and Molly invited her guests over to the terrace for dessert and coffee at ten o'clock. The artist, Roger Finsterman, wandered over from the pigeonnier, his shirt stained with paint.

"That apricot tart looks incredible," he said.

Molly smiled and handed him a knife to cut a slice. She wasn't sure what to make of Finsterman—he spoke politely enough, but he always seemed to be thinking of something else, barely even present. "I hope you're enjoying Castillac? I love this time of year. For one thing—having light this late in the evening is so wonderful!"

Finsterman ate a bite of apricot tart and looked out to the meadow without answering.

With relief Molly heard the chatty Americans, Olive and Josh Mackley, coming around the side of the house. "Hello!" she called out. "Where did your travels take you today?"

"We just got back," Olive said enthusiastically. "We went up to Brantôme today. The guidebooks call it the Venice of the Dordogne, which is absolutely ridiculous since it has virtually nothing to do with Venice. But—it's a charming town and we're glad we went."

"Thanks for having us over," said her husband, cutting pieces of tart and then pouring cups of coffee. "Please tell me this is decaf? If I drink regular coffee at this time of night I'll be up all night."

"Oh, Josh," said his wife, rolling her eyes. "You're so high-maintenance."

Josh rolled his eyes at Molly and gave her a wink.

Bobo barked and ran around the house. Molly thought she might have heard a car in the driveway and figured it was Ben. She hoped he would come out to the terrace but knew he was something of an introvert with little interest in entertaining her guests, and didn't hold it against him.

"Bonsoir Molly!" said Pierre Gault in his deep voice, appearing in the dusky light. He walked towards them slowly and deliberately, as he always did. Pierre never seemed to be in a hurry. "Excuse me for interrupting. I've just now left the Lafont's. It's late but I thought I'd come over to see that barn you were telling me about."

"Would you forgive me?" Molly said to her guests. "Pierre is the best mason in the Dordogne, and he's so in demand it can be very hard to get a few minutes with him."

Finsterman was chewing thoughtfully and still looking out at the meadow, and said nothing. Olive and Josh assured her it was no problem at all as long as she didn't mind risking coming back to an empty tart plate.

"Would you like some?" Molly asked Pierre, but he shook his head, and they went off in search of the crumbling barn.

"The work you did in the pigeonnier has been a smashing success," said Molly, who found Pierre a bit hard to talk to. "Almost everyone has commented on the windows you made out of the nest-boxes. I'm not sure you'll be able to make magic out of this barn—it's such a ruin I didn't even realize it was here until Bobo led me over this way. Pretty sure the realtor didn't know either since it was never mentioned when I was buying La Baraque. You'll see—it looks like a small hill of underbrush more than anything."

"The countryside is littered with broken-down stone buildings," he said. "Some are worth repairing, some not. Have you considered building any new structures for guests?"

"Yes, I've thought about it. But people really seem to love the old buildings—which I understand, I love them too. If I built something new, it would have to stand out somehow—I mean, make a gain in another direction what I would lose by not having the character of the old, you see what I mean?"

Pierre nodded. "I suppose. A gimmick, in other words."

"Yes! Like...gîtes off the grid, or with frescoes, or...or something." She stopped and whistled for Bobo. "It's right over there," she said, pointing at a dark blob in the fading light. "I hope it's not too dark to get an idea."

Pierre waded into the underbrush, then ripped some vines off something that might be a wall. He walked farther, muttering something she couldn't understand, and disappeared into the foliage.

"It's a real wreck!" she called after him.

Molly stood looking around in the half-dark, inhaling the sweet summer air, listening to Pierre crashing around and the night-birds singing. Before long he was back. "Sorry to say—that would be quite a project, Molly. You've only got three walls and no roof, and one of those walls is only about four feet high. To get a really clear idea of what would be involved, I'd have to come back when the light was better and clear off enough of the vines to see the whole thing."

"Oh."

"But the good news is that the part of the wall I got a look at is in decent shape. It was built right, and the stone has held up, as it usually does. Also, it's a big structure, so have you thought about how you would want to use all that space? Do you just want to divide it up into rooms, with a standard kitchen and bath? Possibly two separate gîtes in the same building? Or do you have some other idea?"

"So you're saying you could rebuild it?"

"I can rebuild anything, Molly. The only question is whether it's worth it to you to pay for it."

"When could you start?"

Pierre barked out a sort of laugh and they turned back towards the house. "I won't be done at the Lafont's for another six weeks at least. I'm making a circular stairway out of stone, it's a bit problematic, and the first try didn't work."

"I'll work on the design, and then we'll talk again in a few weeks, maybe you could give me an estimate?"

Pierre nodded.

"It was nice meeting your wife the other night," she said, as Bobo snuffled nearby.

Pierre made a sort of grunt. "See you in a few weeks," he said, and went back around the house to his truck, walking in his slow deliberate way.

"Pierre" means stone in French, thought Molly, watching him go. I can't believe I never put it together that he has the perfect name for a mason.

The guests had disappeared to their dwellings and Molly found an empty terrace save for the orange cat licking up crumbs from the apricot tart.

It was after eleven. She wondered why Ben had never shown up. They hadn't made a plan, but he had been coming over most evenings, and she liked it. She liked *him*. And this life in Castillac —it was turning out to be better than she ever would have imagined.

4

Iris Gault finished cutting up the potatoes and slid them into a huge pot of boiling water. It was the last day of school, and while she was happy to be getting off work for a few months, she always missed the children terribly. She checked her watch, always careful to time the cooking so the food would be ready all at once, and then stepped into the bathroom and used a paper towel to wipe the steam from her face.

The mirror over the sink was old and not perfectly clean. Iris looked at herself. She was forty-four and unhappy. She understood this was a common enough state for people of her age—the sudden realization like a thump to the side of the head that the end of life was zooming ever closer...and there she was, wasting time, still waiting for the good part to begin.

Her marriage was no comfort.

She still had her looks, she could admit that to herself, though she guessed their days were distinctly numbered. For a while, when she was young, she had believed that her beauty had significance somehow—that it was a kind of good luck that meant she was going to have an extraordinary life. There was no one she could talk to about these feelings, since, understandably, even her best friends did not want to hear about such things. But—briefly —the world had seemed so welcoming, so happy to have her in it! Where had that feeling gone?

Iris ran a finger down her nose, looking at herself in the spotty mirror. She wiped under both eyes to catch some errant flakes of eyeliner.

What now, she asked herself. What am I going to do now?

"Iris!" her co-worker Ada was banging on the bathroom door. "Don't mean to disturb you but the purée? It's gotten too thick and sticking to the bottom of the pans."

"Take it off the heat," said Iris through the door. And then she took a deep breath and held it until she was uncomfortable, and squeezed her eyes shut. Turning the cold water on hard, she put her face under the tap and shivered at the cold.

Leaving the bathroom without another glance in the mirror, she appraised the situation in the kitchen to see if they were on schedule for lunch. A big man in blue coveralls came in the back door, his hands and face shiny with plumber's grease. "Madame Gault," he said, "I don't know what you or Ada is putting down that sink, but I can't keep the thing clear if you keep on like that."

Iris sighed. She suspected that Hector himself was putting something down the sink just for an excuse to come into the kitchen and bother them.

"I will speak to Ada and make every effort," she said. "What was it this time?"

"A wadded-up rag, that's what!" said Hector. He flexed his shoulders and looked intently into Iris's eyes. "What's a pretty girl like you doing in the kitchen, anyways? Don't your husband take care of you?"

"Oh, Hector," laughed Iris. "None of that is your concern. I'm very happy in my job. Thank you for fixing the sink and now I've got to get lunch served, the children will be here any moment."

She directed Ada and the others until the tables were set and all the food—baguettes with butter, courgette and potato purée, pork, salad—was ready. They could hear the laughter and clamoring of the first group of students on their way to the cantine, and Iris glanced at the tables to make sure they were set properly: glasses, cutlery, napkins. Lunch was serious business and considered part of a child's education; they practiced not only using knives and forks but also conversation, guided by their teachers and occasionally their principal.

"Bonjour, Iris," said Caroline, smiling as she held the door for the children. "I've brought Madame Poirier's class today—she just went home with a headache."

"That's a shame, and no way to start vacation," said Iris brightly. "Samuel, I have your very favorite cheese today!" She reached out and touched the boy's shoulder as he went by, grinning at her. "Eveline! *Mousse au chocolat* for dessert!"

Eveline shrieked and the two girls whose hands she was holding shrieked in response, and they danced in a circle singing a song with *"mousse au chocolat"* as the only lyric.

"You have any summer plans?" asked Caroline, once her charges were all seated at their tables.

Iris shrugged. "Who knows?" She watched the children scrambling into their seats and felt a pang of missing them in advance. "I feel like a big change, Caro. Maybe I will go to Mozambique!"

Caroline looked startled at Iris's sudden vehemence. The other classes were led in by their teachers, the children louder than usual from the excitement of having their last lunch of the school year. Tristan Séverin came in just as they were beginning to eat, his pants a little too short for his long legs and a swipe of black marker on his cheek.

"Students!" he cried, and miraculously, they quieted down to listen. "I want first for you all to say thank you to Madame Gault for feeding you so well all year—"

"MERCI MADAME GAULT!" shouted the whole room with glee. Iris smiled and nodded, twisting her braid in her fingers.

"—and then I want you to thank Mademoiselle Dubois for all

her work in the office and making sure the buses went where they were supposed to—"

"MERCI MADEMOISELLE DUBOIS!"

Caroline made a bow and waved.

"—and then...well, what about me?" said Principal Séverin, and the children laughed before screaming their thanks to him as well.

After the meal was over and everyone had left but the staff at the cantine, Iris was tempted to go back into the bathroom just to have a moment's privacy. As soon as the kitchen was cleaned and straightened, her vacation would start. She had no plan, no solid ideas, nothing but a nearly feverish desire to change her life somehow—to go somewhere, to start over, to shake everything up and begin again.

֍

AFTER ANOTHER DAY of scraping wallpaper and working in the garden, Molly wanted to go to Chez Papa and see friends. Ben was deep in a book about the Napoleonic Wars and so Molly rode her scooter into the village alone.

"Madame Sutton is in the house!" said Lawrence Weebly, seeing her stop to chat with someone in the doorway. Molly grinned and waved, then came over to kiss cheeks.

"What's the news?" she asked, always ready for a juicy bit of gossip, and knowing Weebly to be not just a good source, but the best.

"I've got nothing," he said, holding up his hands. "I've never seen the village so quiet and well-behaved. As far as I can tell, Castillac for the moment is the epicenter of contentment and honest living."

"For the moment," said Molly.

"We should be glad."

"But we're not," she whispered, and they both laughed. "Hey Nico!"

"Kir coming right up," he said, breaking away from a conversation at the other end of the bar.

"Frances coming tonight?"

"I think so," Nico answered, glowering. "She's a little hard to pin down."

Molly laughed. "Yep! That's our Frances all right. Don't take it personally, Nico."

He shrugged.

"Trouble in paradise?" asked Lawrence.

"Eh, wherever Frances goes, there's trouble. You know I love her like a sister, but I'd kill myself before getting romantically involved with her. She's...unreliable."

"Ah," said Lawrence. "I'm not shocked to hear that. But still, no doubt it's that very unreliability that attracts our Nico? Frances is unpredictable and a little mysterious. He can't become complacent. That's alluring, am I right? Not that I have experience in these matters," he added, looking away.

Molly shrugged. "I guess so. For sure, if what you want is cozy nights watching television together, Frances is not your girl. Last week she drove all over the Dordogne looking for vintage clothing because she got it in her head to dress up as an heiress from the Belle Époque."

"Did she find what she was looking for?"

"It's safe to say Frances almost never finds what she is looking for," laughed Molly. "Which is probably the point. Anyway, she unearthed a moth-eaten skirt with a bustle but that was it. I think the fever has passed though, so she won't be driving to Bordeaux or Paris trying to complete the outfit."

"She's an heiress for real, have I got that right?" asked Lawrence, *sotto voce*, after a long sip of his Negroni.

"Yes. Well, maybe. Her family has truckloads of money, that's for sure. Something industrial, I believe, that the great-grandfather did. But they try to hold that money over Frances's head, possibly cutting her out of the will entirely—not that it makes any difference to her. She went out and made her own money long ago, so the family shenanigans don't affect her much."

"Good for her," said Lawrence raising his glass. "To independence!"

Molly raised hers, as did others down the bar, who pronounced "independence" pretty well for people who spoke little English.

"Well bonsoir, Pierre, we so rarely have the pleasure!" said Lawrence, speaking over Molly's shoulder to the mason as he came into the bar. "And the second appearance in one week!"

"Bonsoir Lawrence, Molly," said Pierre Gault. "Whiskey," he said to Nico. And then he stood still, looking at himself in the mirror behind the bar, biting his lower lip with some ferocity.

"Did you just finish up at the Lafont's?" asked Molly. "How are the circular stairs going?"

For a moment Molly and Lawrence were not sure Pierre had heard her. Then he turned to her, another long pause went by, and he managed to say, "Yes, just left. It's a big job. I'm not sure when I'll be free to start your barn."

Molly was a little taken aback since he seemed to be answering a question she had not asked. "No rush," she said finally. "I probably shouldn't do it anyway, not this year. It's sometimes hard to know how quickly to put my profits back into the business," she said, looking from Pierre to Lawrence.

"The usual advice is to have a decent-sized nest-egg first, especially since your income is on the unpredictable side," said Lawrence. "You don't want to have a bad couple of months and not have money for operating expenses. Or anything to eat."

Molly sighed. "Well, sure. A nest-egg. That would be the safe path, wouldn't it? And I do have a nest-egg going, it's just…small. Pierre, I'll have to see your estimate first of course, but unless it's way higher than I expect, I'll want you to go ahead with it. Once I can get capacity over ten guests at once, I think my situation will be a lot more secure. I'm willing to take some risks to get there."

Lawrence shrugged, knowing that Molly would do whatever she wanted no matter what advice she was given— and it was something he liked about her. Indecisive she was not.

Pierre stood between them like a statue, still looking at himself in the mirror, which Molly thought was a bit strange since he had never once struck her as the narcissistic type. She considered asking if anything was wrong, but decided it was too nosy a question even for her, since he was a very private sort of man.

Later, she fervently wished she *had* asked, but of course by then it was too late.

5

The children of the village school were blissfully *en vacances*. Though she missed their high spirits and happy noise, Caroline was looking forward to bringing some real order to Tristan Séverin's office now that the pressure of the school year was finished. She was dressed in her customary crisp white shirt and tailored skirt, paired with low heels—a flattering, professional outfit. She wore little makeup, but hardly anyone would say it was missed, as her bone structure was striking and her color lively.

She did not see Tristan's car in the small lot for the school. She often teased him about being lazy for driving, since he and his wife lived in the village and he certainly could have walked. But Tristan insisted that his car was his refuge, the one place he could sit and have a private moment to think, and would not be deterred from using it nearly every day.

Caroline opened the door to the school and let herself in, leaving it unlocked behind her. The school building was newish and modern, with large windows in the corridors and rooms that let in plenty of light. One of the things she liked about her job was that the school was positioned in the center of Castillac so it was convenient to everything, and easy to meet up with a friend for lunch if she didn't have duty in the cantine that day.

For a person who liked to organize, having an entire day with nothing else pressing to attend to was bliss itself. She settled at her desk to run through any emails that needed her attention, and made short work of those. Then she took the first stack of files and papers from Tristan's desk and sat down to deal with them. She did not drink coffee or tea because she did not like to mix work with food or drink.

An hour, then two, slipped by. Caroline made her way through that stack and then another. How satisfying it was to see the top of Tristan's desk coming into view! She hoped he would be pleased and surprised when he saw how much she had accomplished.

Absorbed in a thick document about a proposed curriculum change for the second graders, Caroline startled mildly when she heard footsteps in the corridor. She glanced out of the expansive window and saw the florist's van parked in the small school parking area.

"*Coucou!*" called the delivery man for Madame Langevin's florist shop.

"Bonjour," said Caroline, jumping up from her desk as he appeared in the doorway holding a large bouquet.

"Here you are!" he said. "Big day for flowers for some reason. More deliveries, I have to run!"

"All right, thanks very much," said Caroline, not allowing herself to hope they were for her, since she had no one in her life who would be sending her such a magnificent bouquet—or any bouquet, for that matter.

The arrangement was primarily roses, pinks and a few light reds, with blue irises artistically placed among them. The rounded rose blossoms made a pleasing contrast with the spikes of the irises, the colors blended perfectly...all in all, the work of someone who knew flowers and what to do with them.

Caroline leaned her nose into a rose and inhaled, knowing that roses from the florist were almost always without fragrance since stamina was the more important quality. But this rose, a cabbagey pink, had a delicate perfume that made Caroline smile wistfully.

The small envelope clipped to a plastic stem simply said "Tristan."

She stood thinking about his calendar, wondering whether she had forgotten his birthday or some event that she should have remembered. Why in the world would someone have sent her boss a bouquet like this? Caroline wondered for a moment and then sat back down at her desk and reopened the document on the curriculum change.

Suddenly, quickly, before she had a chance to change her mind, she stood up and approached the bouquet. She paused for a second. Then she plucked the small envelope from among the leaves and opened it. She read it. Her face instantly flushed and a sensation of watery weakness ran through her body.

How could he do this to me! she thought, the words like a scream inside her head. Caroline read the note again, her hands trembling with fury. She let loose the filthiest series of expletives she could think of, though ordinarily she never used that kind of language. Then, after taking a deep breath to calm herself down a little, she eased the card into its small envelope and clipped it back to the stem among the glossy green leaves.

Caroline didn't know what to do next. She looked rather wildly around the office, as though hoping something she saw would give her direction. She noticed the bare spot on Tristan's desk but it gave her no joy, not now.

Finally she picked up her handbag and left, locking the door of the school behind her, and fled for home. It was ten blocks away but her heels were comfortable. She prayed she would not run into anyone she knew because she felt unable to master her emotions.

How could he?

Caroline rented a small apartment in an old building on rue

Tartine. It suited her quite well as she could walk easily to work, and the other apartments in the building were rented by women roughly her age. She used to have a drink regularly with Adèle Faure, before she moved out a few months ago, and though she knew the others less well, they were still friends of a sort. They shared the work of a simple garden in the backyard, split up the electricity bills without arguing, and got on without incident.

She walked quickly, on the verge of running, the intense assortment of feelings she was in the grip of not diminishing as she got closer to home. Caroline wrenched open the door and ran up the creaky old stairs to her rooms. Without hesitation she went to the kitchen cabinet, took out a plate, and hurled it to the floor.

She took out another and flung it into the wall. Porcelain shattered, sending splinters in a wide spray. Caroline kept going, picking up plate after plate and throwing them with as much force as she could muster, in every direction but the windows.

When she had no more plates, she sank to the floor, put her head in her hands, and sobbed.

EDMOND NUGENT LIKED order in his life. His work schedule was ruled by the demands of dough and baking times, and he had followed the same routine—making the same things at the same times every day, every week—for years. It suited him. He appreciated that his customers also had their habits: most of his regulars tended to come into Pâtisserie Bujold at the same time of day, buy the same pastries, even exchange the same flavor of small talk.

So Nugent was a bit disturbed that Thursday when Caroline Dubois appeared at the shop early in the morning, when usually she came in the afternoons, after school let out. Thankfully she asked for the same strawberry tart she always got, so all was not chaos. But nevertheless he could see that something was very wrong.

"Mademoiselle," he said gently, "I don't mean to overstep, but you seem...you seem to be in some distress. Is there anything I can do?"

An uncharacteristic expression of contempt blazed on Caroline's pretty face. "No, Monsieur Nugent. I don't think there is anything at all anyone can do." She fished in her purse for the correct change, and then a wicked idea occurred to her, which, also uncharacteristically, she acted on without hesitating.

"I believe you are friends with Iris Gault?" she said, her tone changing to nonchalant, though Nugent was not fooled by it.

"Yes, Mademoiselle," said Nugent. "We have known each other for many years." He couldn't keep his mouth from spreading into a smile at the thought of Iris.

"It's too bad, really, isn't it?"

"What's too bad?" asked Nugent, feeling prickles of warning on the back of his neck.

"Too bad about the affair she's having with Monsieur Séverin."

"Mon—" gasped Nugent. He turned away, straightening up a stack of napkins on the counter behind him. His throat felt like it was closing up. "I don't think—"

"Oh, I have proof," Caroline said. "I'll admit I was as surprised as you. Granted, everyone knows Madame Séverin has her problems...."

"Depression is a kind of monster," said Nugent, his voice faint. They stood looking at each other but lost in their own particular wretchedness. "Well, it's none of my business anyway."

"Nor mine," said Caroline, and took the bag with her strawberry tart and banged out the door.

Nugent put his palms on the counter and leaned his weight into them. Iris, with *Tristan?* He couldn't believe it. Tristan had always seemed a pleasant enough fellow. Coffee éclair, liked raspberries if they were fresh. But a bit of a goofball. And married to

that poor Lucie, who had been suffering so terribly from depression for years. He couldn't remember the last time he'd seen her,
now that he thought about it.

Iris with Tristan? Nugent just could not believe it. He doesn't
have enough passion, thought the pastry chef, drawing himself up.
Tristan is not worthy of a goddess such as Iris Gault!

And neither is that Pierre, he added darkly. Oh Iris, you
exceptional, magnificent creature! Why not me? Why not *me?*

AS NUGENT HAD a strict schedule for his entire day, bedtime was
no different. Eight o'clock at the very latest, and preferably seven.
But here it was, getting close to nine—nine!—and instead of
climbing into bed with a cup of chamomile tea, Nugent was
pacing from his bedroom to the kitchen, muttering to himself.

Tristan Séverin was a puerile sort of fellow, a *lightweight*. He
did not in any way deserve to have Iris Gault in his bed. Sure, he
had his charms, Nugent supposed grudgingly. The parents of
schoolchildren seemed to approve of him. But that's just it—he's
boyish. Exactly suitable for a job in a school. But a woman like
Iris...deserves a man.

Nugent had been going around and around like this for several
hours. While still at the shop, he had marginally been able to
distract himself with all the work and dealing with customers that
the shop required, but once he was home, the torrents of jealousy
just kept coming and coming.

Why did she never choose me?

They had been in school together, as children. Grown up
together. Nugent had watched the quiet, pretty girl transform
into a beauty, as simultaneously he became a man. But she had
never allowed him so much as a kiss. Not once.

He put on his nightshirt and got into bed, and the instant his
head hit the pillow he was filled with a kind of rage unknown to

him before that moment. Throwing the summer coverlet aside, he leapt out of bed and got dressed.

Something had to be done. He could not bear these feelings, not for another second. It was time for Edmond Nugent, at long last, to act.

❦ 6 ❦

I ris knelt by a parterre outlined in miniature English boxwood. The shrub grew very slowly so it didn't often need her attention, and that evening she let her hands drift over the top of it, releasing its distinctive scent, and then leaned over to ferret out some weeds that were trying to advance into the santolina and lavender which she had planted in a large sunburst design.

It was dusk. Pierre was still at work, as he almost always was. It was one of Iris's favorite times in the garden—the light was soft and she could hear animals scurrying about in the woods close by. The birds were singing their hearts out and the sound expanded her sense of melancholy, but in a way that felt more pleasurable than not. She was not working with any sort of fervor but kept sitting back and breathing in the perfume of her garden, the roses and oriental lilies, and watching the birds flit in the trees, and the clouds lit up by the sinking sun.

That night, as she pulled weeds and fussed over the topiary swans, she made a decision. She was realizing, rather late at age forty-four, that she had allowed her life to drift, allowed other people to make important decisions for her, allowed their desires to supplant her own. It was no wonder she was unhappy when she had taken so little responsibility for herself. She saw, finally, that she had expected happiness to come to her and not to have to seek it.

Marrying a man simply because he wanted her so desperately —how could she ever have thought that would go well?

On the side of one of the swans was a knotty stem that continually caused trouble. For some reason, new growth sprouted from it in great profusion and in all directions, and if the smooth lines of the swan's wing was to be preserved, Iris had to clip the soft new growth from it nearly every week. She was absorbed in this task when someone came around the side of the house, walking slowly on the gravel path.

She heard the footsteps, and looked up. "Bonsoir," she said with a weary smile, letting the hand with the clippers drop to her side.

※ 7 ※

Gilles Maron, acting chief gendarme of Castillac, had been having a decent summer so far. A little on the boring side, since his day-to-day had mainly consisted of rounding up drunk drivers and dealing with a few break-ins of vacation homes in which nothing much was taken. But Maron had discovered during the last murder investigation that he was an uneasy leader, and that somehow being made acting chief had undermined his former confidence in his own judgment. He was hoping he only needed more experience before being in charge would feel comfortable, and he hadn't minded a few months of quiet in the village while he got his feet more firmly underneath him.

That Friday in July was the first day on the job for Thérèse Perrault's replacement. A man, for which Maron was grateful, being more comfortable in the company of men. But so far, unfortunately, not a man he especially liked.

Officer Paul-Henri Monsour was young and untested. He had grown up in an upper-middle class suburb of Paris, and wasted no time letting Maron know that the Monsour family thought being a gendarme was socially beneath them.

"I'm heading home," said Maron in early evening, after an uneventful day. "When your shift is over, lock up the station as I showed you. It's been quiet lately so I doubt you'll have any problems, but if anything happens, you know where to reach me." Maron flexed his shoulders, could think of nothing else to say, and left the station.

Monsour smiled a wide, toothy smile once he was alone. He had dreamed of being a gendarme since he was a little boy, and here he was at his first posting, all by himself and in charge on his very first day at work. He got up from his desk and straightened up, placing chairs along the wall in a neat line and sweeping the big room where his desk was and where people first came inside. How could Maron let the place get so filthy? he wondered, going to the bathroom for paper towels so he could wipe down the dust on the windowsills.

His paperwork was all taken care of, and he hadn't been there long enough to have anything on his desk that needed attending to. The big clock on the wall—hopelessly old-fashioned, Monsour thought—ticked away, counting off the minutes of his shift.

There was nothing to do.

Calls could be diverted from the station to his cell, so it wasn't absolutely necessary that he stay inside—Maron had told him it was all right, even helpful, to walk around the village while on duty, alert to the needs of the villagers (and perhaps the villagers' pets). So after carefully locking the station door behind him, Monsour set out into the warm July night, thinking to acquaint himself with the narrow streets and learn his way around a bit. With any luck, he'd find someone who needed help, or even better, someone who needed to be put back in line.

He found his way to the Place easily enough. A statue of a World War I soldier stood in the center, ringed by flowers. A crowd was spilling out of Chez Papa and he heard a woman's high laugh. A well-dressed couple went into a restaurant farther along, a group of teenagers went into the Presse, and a chubby chihuahua with a red collar crossed the street after looking both ways.

Pretty enough village, he thought. In his mind Castillac was only a stepping-stone of his career, a short-lived posting on his way to where the action was. He expected before long to be working in the outskirts of Paris, rooting out terrorist cells—and the sooner he was done in Castillac, the better. Monsour wanted danger, excitement, and the possibility of quick advancement. He wanted to be where he would risk taking a contraband bullet anytime he stepped outside…and none of that, clearly, had a thing to do with this sleepy, wholesome village, far from any city.

When his cell buzzed he quickly pressed it to his ear.

"Maron?" said a man's voice.

"This is Officer Monsour. What's the problem?"

"Where is Maron?"

"I am on duty now, Monsieur. It is my first day on the Castillac force."

"I see. Well, my wife's been hurt. I've called the ambulance but I guess you should come too."

Monsour's heart began to race. "What's your address, Monsieur?"

"67 route de Canard. Stone house, on the west side of the road. A dark blue Ford in the driveway."

"On my way. Is your wife…is she all right, sir?"

"I don't believe so, no," said Pierre Gault, and the two men hung up without saying anything further.

❧ 8 ❧

The Gault's house on route de Canard was right on the edge of the village. Set back from the road, and made of yellow limestone, the building was hidden by a high evergreen hedge. The house number was marked clearly on the postal box and gendarme Jean-Henri Monsour had no problem finding it. He was on foot, Maron having failed to show him where the keys to the police vehicle or the scooter were kept.

Monsour had no idea what to expect. He had never approached a situation such as this by himself and had so little general experience that he believed the possibilities of what he might find were nearly endless. He didn't know what kind of shape the woman was in, whether the man who called had hurt her or if there had been an accident. The ambulance wasn't in the driveway, and as he walked up the driveway, he heard no sounds except for the nightbirds and a single car heading out of town on route de Canard.

With some trepidation Monsour knocked on the heavy old door. He realized that he had failed to ask the caller's name and had no idea whose house this was.

"*Excusez-moi! Il y a quelqu'un?*" he shouted, banging harder when no one appeared.

He heard slow footsteps from within. Then someone fiddling with the door handle.

"Salut," said a large man, opening the door at last. "Thank you for coming. No idea what's keeping the ambulance."

Monsour stood uncomfortably on the doorstep. "May I come in?" he asked finally.

"Oh yes, of course," said Pierre.

"I am Officer Monsour," he said, remembering that he had already told the man his name when they spoke on the phone but the man had not given his. "Where is your wife?"

"She's in the kitchen. Down that corridor," he said, gesturing for the officer to go ahead.

The house was neatly kept. Monsour passed the living room and glanced in to see everything tidy and clean. A stack of books stood on a small table by an armchair. An empty teacup by the books.

Monsour blinked hard when he got far enough down the corridor to see into the kitchen where Iris lay on her side, one arm outstretched, her legs bent at the knees as though she were running.

Her eyes open wide.

Monsour took a deep breath, strode into the kitchen, and knelt by the body. He placed two fingers on her neck, looking for her carotid artery, but not with any real hope he would feel a pulse. She was lying right at the bottom of a curving, narrow set of stairs.

"I'm sorry," he said to Pierre, as he stood up. "You said you called the ambulance? How long ago?"

"Oh, it was…I can't say, really. It's not like I look at my watch whenever I do anything."

"What is your name, Monsieur?"

"Pierre. Pierre Gault." He walked to the sink and looked out the window at the garden.

"I wish it were otherwise, Monsieur Gault, but I'm afraid I have to call the coroner."

Pierre nodded. He was chewing on his lower lip, scanning the garden as though looking for something. He said nothing.

With a sense of importance, Monsour called Florian Nagrand on his cell and told him the Gault address. "Broken neck, looks like," he added, irritating Nagrand, who never liked it when gendarmes waded into his bailiwick.

It was uncomfortable being alone in the kitchen with a dead woman, especially since her husband showed no signs of grief, or any emotion at all. Monsour looked around the kitchen but there was not much to see: everything was put away, there were no dishes in the sink, no half-eaten meal on the table, no sense that normal life had just been interrupted. He appreciated order and cleanliness to a fairly high degree, yet the Gault house, as far as Monsour had been able to see, was so orderly that it felt almost as though people didn't actually live there.

"Is there anyone I can call for you?" asked Monsour. "Relative, friend, anyone?"

Pierre shook his head.

Monsour looked out of the window over the sink, wondering what he was looking at, and saw a rather elaborate garden, lit up with artfully-placed floodlights—parterres, a grand potager, and even some topiary swans—and a small shed back towards the woods.

"You like to garden?" asked Monsour.

"No," said Pierre. A long pause. "That was my wife."

"Well, it's quite impressive. Must have been a lot of back-breaking work to make something like that."

Pierre shrugged. "I never understood the point. It all dies, you see. Not like making something that lasts."

Monsour thought about saying that we all die, so what was the point of anything, but he had the good manners to keep his mouth shut. "I'm sorry for not covering up your wife, but that is protocol, until the coroner gives the okay."

"I understand," said Pierre, turning away from the window and looking down at Iris for the first time that Monsour saw.

Monsour watched his face, but was unable to get any idea at all about what the man was feeling or thinking as he gazed on the broken body of his wife.

"Were you home? Any idea what might have happened?" asked the gendarme.

Pierre looked up at him sharply. "She fell down the stairs," he said, with an edge of contempt. "I thought that was fairly plain."

"Yes, of course," said Monsour hurriedly. "But Monsieur... people use stairs all the time. Many times a day. And for the most part we do it without uneasiness. An accident such as this—it's likely to have another aspect, if you understand me. For example, is it possible that your wife had more to drink this evening than usual? Something that might have affected her balance or control of her physical self?"

"Oh *bon sang*," said Pierre, leaving the kitchen by the back door, and letting it bang shut behind him.

Monsour's hands clenched into fists. The man had a lot of nerve, walking away in the middle of being questioned. And with a dead wife on the kitchen floor!

He wrenched open the back door and followed him, expecting that Gault would be going to the front of the house, looking out for the ambulance. But Gault was walking into his wife's garden, pacing slowly and deliberately down the gravel path.

Had he pushed his wife down the stairs? If so, why was he not making more of an effort to look less guilty?

And where, for God's sake, was Maron?

"YOU'RE PUTTING it right over the window!"

"Relax, Franny, I know what I'm doing," Molly lied, as she lined up the pattern of the second wallpaper roll to match the small green leaves on the first, already neatly glued to the wall. She smoothed it with a sponge and stepped back. "Now watch this." She took a single-edged razor blade and cut the excess from around the window molding, and within seconds, that section of wall looked perfectly papered.

"You really do know what you're doing," murmured Franny from her usual position on the bed. "I like your new pattern. I mean, *I* don't like it, but I think for guests it was a good choice. Tasteful and inoffensive."

"You hate it."

"Of course."

"I sort of like it. I know it's sort of corny English countryside and all, but I just like leaves."

"I thought you liked roses."

"I like leaves *and* roses. I wish I could remember the name of that movie with the faded rose wallpaper. A handsome stranger—charming of course—rents a room in an old woman's house. Maybe she was running a hotel, I can't remember. The old woman is in a wheelchair." Molly paused as she ran the roller dipped in glue along the back of the third section of wallpaper, spread on the floor. "Don't you think old women in wheelchairs ought to be exempt from horror movies?"

"Haha!" hooted Frances. "You're just fixated on that movie because you rent your rooms to charming, handsome strangers."

Molly laughed. "Like Wesley Addison?"

Her cell, sitting on the bedside table, made a whooshing sound. "Will you check that for me? Anything I have to deal with?"

Frances rolled over and picked up the phone.

"It's from Lawrence. Just says: *possible murder. call me.*"

Molly looked at Frances with wide eyes. "What?" she said, incredulous.

"You've lured me to a hotbed of homicide," said Frances, taking another sip of lemonade and flopping onto her back. "I admit I get bored easily, but this might be going too far even for me."

Molly juggled the third roll up, adjusted it so the seams matched the second, and pressed it into place. "Oh God," she said. "I was having so much fun, doing this wallpaper. I was thinking I might wallpaper the whole house, maybe the cottage too. It's so satisfying, you know? Covers up everything with pretty leaves. No big emotions, no hurt, no danger. Just...wallpaper."

Frances held out the phone. Molly took it and then stopped for a moment, first to pray that it wasn't anyone she knew, and then feeling bad because whoever it was, that person had loved ones, whether she was among them or not.

Lawrence picked up after the first ring.

"What the hell?" said Molly.

"I know. And it's especially bad this time. Someone well-liked."

"Well, don't be coy, tell me who!"

"Iris Gault."

Molly stood with her mouth open, thoughts racing.

"Who?" asked Frances, leaning in next to the phone at Molly's ear.

"Iris Gault," Molly said to her.

"That's right," said Lawrence. "Are you ready to get to work?"

"Get to work?"

"Pierre is going to need considerable help. Apparently she was pushed down the stairs and he called the authorities. As I'm sure you know, it's almost always the husband in these sorts of cases."

"Pushed down the stairs? How do you know she didn't just fall?"

"She might have. The coroner is at the house now, making a determination."

"How *do* you get your information?"

Lawrence laughed lightly. "I'm just saying, if Pierre doesn't have a rock-solid alibi, I fear for him, I really do."

"It's hardly my job to...."

"Look, Molly—Ben is off the force. And Maron is...not completely incompetent, but not the best, you would agree? Thérèse is gone. I haven't met the new fellow yet, but from where I'm sitting, you're the best qualified detective in the village. So tally ho, my dear. I've got to run. Keep in touch."

Molly let the phone drop and slowly sat down on the bed.

"I just spent the other night talking to Iris," said Frances. "I liked her. I really liked her."

"She had incredible eyes."

"Absolutely gorgeous woman. And interesting to talk to. Way more interesting than her husband, who as far as I can tell, talks about nothing but rocks."

"I don't know, I think Lawrence might be getting ahead of himself," said Molly. "Okay, she fell down the stairs. Broke her neck, I guess. But that could happen to anyone. Doesn't automatically have to be murder, right?"

Frances nodded. "Right. I've read that more people die falling down the stairs than you'd ever believe. Probably most of them are blotto, though."

Molly picked at a cuticle on her thumb. "I just...I mean, gosh, I know how it is to be in a bad marriage. I know how it sucks. But that's what divorce is for! Why go to all the trouble and risk of killing someone to get away from them when it's so easy to accomplish that another way?"

"A million reasons, Molly, you know that. For insurance money, inheritance money, revenge...the list is practically endless. Can you imagine how satisfying it would be to murder a person who had been chewing with his mouth open at the breakfast table for twenty years?"

"Or clipping his toenails in bed?"

"Picking his teeth. Being OCD about everything. Opening your mail. Giving orders. Wearing ugly shirts. Never, ever closing a kitchen cabinet."

Molly laughed. "How in the world does anyone ever stay married?"

"You're asking the wrong person, darlin'."

"Well, I'm thinking this source of Lawrence's might have got it wrong this time. I'm terribly sorry about Iris—not to make it all about me, but I think we'd have been good friends. I just don't see where a fall down the stairs equals murder."

Frances shrugged. "We'll just have to see what the coroner says. He any good?"

"Never met him. Ben seems to think he's okay. Never heard any complaints at least. I wonder how—or if—he'll be able to tell whether she was pushed or not?"

"Physics."

"Never my best subject."

"Good thing you're not the coroner."

"Help me with this next section of wallpaper, will you? I swear you're the worst helper ever."

"Can't we have lunch? Who knew that once you became a business owner you'd turn into such a slave driver."

Molly agreed that lunch was a good idea. As she straightened up the wallpaper project, capping the glue and bringing the roller downstair to rinse off, she thought about Iris Gault. About her melancholy blue-green eyes, her voluptuous figure, and the streaks of gray in her thick hair.

If someone did kill you, we'll find out who, Molly promised her, even though at the same time she was insisting to herself that the death was almost certainly an accident.

9

That night Molly tried to convince Ben to join her at Chez Papa. "Come on, won't you come with me? It's more fun when you're there. Plus you know more people and can find out stuff I won't be able to."

"Not only is Iris not my case," said Ben. "We haven't even heard the coroner's report. The fall may well have been an accident." Ben walked to the refrigerator and opened it. "I certainly hope it was. What is this obsession you have with lemonade?"

"Nice try. I don't get distracted that easily."

"I mean, I like lemonade well enough. Everyone likes lemonade. But for me it is better as an occasional thing. Although perhaps I will splash a little into a glass of Prosecco."

"Do people think you're a traitor, a Frenchman drinking Italian wine?"

"Depends on whom you ask. Would you like one?"

"No thank you. And I haven't forgotten what we're talking about. All I want to do is go to Chez Papa, have a drink, and see what people are saying. Maybe someone was with Pierre and he has a good alibi. Wouldn't you be relieved to find that out?"

"Molly, you're burning the step."

"Huh?"

Ben held up the bottle of Prosecco while he thought a moment. "Let's see...no idea what the English idiom is. I mean to say, you're rushing. Skipping over things."

"Ah! Jumping the gun!"

"Precisely. Until I hear from Nagrand how Iris died, I am going to assume her death was an accident." He corked the Prosecco and put it back in the refrigerator. "She was a complicated woman, Iris."

Molly cocked her head. She had thought Iris so stunning that she couldn't imagine any man not being besotted with her, and she felt a ridiculous throb of jealousy at the idea that Ben was thinking about her.

"In what way?"

"Eh, we can talk about it later. I know you're anxious to get to Chez Papa and hear the opinions of everyone at the bar. And in any case, even if Nagrand does end up ruling her death a homicide, I'm leaving this up to the Castillac force."

"But five minutes ago, you *were* the Castillac force!"

"Right—*past tense*. Many months ago now. And I don't regret resigning for one instant, and will not be trying to worm my way into this case, undermining Maron and the new guy, whatever his name is."

"Therese's replacement is already here?"

"Apparently. I don't know any details, not even a name." Ben took a sip of his drink. "This is very good. Sure you don't want one before you go?"

"What are you going to do tonight then?"

"I plan to dive deep into the Napoleonic Wars. I understand you do not share that particular interest, but I can think of nothing more pleasurable than staying here with Bobo and reading for as many hours as I please, lost in the world of 1805. Is it all right with you if I stay here while you're gone?"

"Of course. Don't feed Bobo too many treats." Molly gave up

trying to convince him, knowing that trying to crowbar him out of the house would only make him more resistant. Quickly she changed, put on a swipe of lipstick, and took her beloved scooter into the village.

The mood in Chez Papa was markedly different than it had been the evening before. Though the weather was just as perfect and Alphonse's colored lights twinkled, conversations were muted. There was no laughter, no merriment. Pierre was not a popular man, but his work was respected, and Iris had been the cherished friend of many, as well as the object of much admiration by both men and women. The bad news, coming out of nowhere in what had been such a lovely carefree July, had everyone depressed and even a little nervous.

"Might be your standard homicidal maniac, just passing through," said a man down the bar, but he was shouted down quickly.

"It's actually rare to be murdered by a stranger," said another man, who slammed his beer glass on the bar and nodded to Nico for another.

"I always said beauty like hers is a kind of curse," said Lapin, cradling a glass of house red. "Salut, Molly," he added as she came in, his voice absent its usual jollity.

"Salut, Lapin. Nico."

Nico moved to pour Molly a kir while she kissed cheeks with Lapin. "Did you know Iris?" he asked.

"No, I'd just met her last week, actually, here at Chez Papa. We talked for a few minutes, that was it. She seemed...sad. Was that unusual?"

"I was just saying that she appeared to be taking middle age rather hard," said Lapin. "Her mother died last year, whom she was very close to."

Lawrence Weebly came through the door looking uncharacteristically disheveled.

"Salut, Lawrence," said Molly. "Did you get rolled in the alley?"

"Ah well," said Lawrence, after greeting everyone. He tucked in his shirt and rolled his sleeves up neatly. "I'm devastated by the news. Just devastated. What in the world has happened to our little village?"

"It's not like it's anything new," said the man at the bar, who had already put a big dent in his next glass of beer. "Husband kills wife. End of story."

"That's not much of a story," murmured Molly.

"Pierre's a friend of mine," said another man. "Maybe it looks bad, but I don't think there's any way he's guilty."

"How was their marriage?" Molly asked.

"Eh, marriage," said the beer-drinker. "Who hasn't wanted to kill the person they're married to, more than once? I know I have."

"I think they were happy enough," said Lawrence. "But you know, it's hard to say. Nobody knows what really goes on in the privacy of people's homes."

"To Iris!" said the beer-drinker, and everyone raised a glass and drank to her memory.

Another member of the community was gone, and for a moment everyone at Chez Papa felt a sharp pang of wondering if they too would be hurried off the stage before their time, and if so, would they be next?

10

B en had stayed up very late reading and taken his scooter back to his place almost in the middle of the night, after Molly was long asleep. The next morning was Saturday, Changeover Day, so Molly got up early and went into the village for a quick spin around the market and to get pastries for her guests' final breakfast. She did rather miss being able to take her time on Saturday, talking to the vendors and anyone else she came across—but since Saturday was really the only day she had to work hard, she couldn't really complain.

First to Raoul, the pig farmer, for a brief discussion about politics and some of his beloved sausages. Then to the spice man, where she bought a variety of Thai spices thinking she might try a curry sometime that week. Then to her friend Manette, who reigned over the largest and most impressive display of vegetables.

"Bonjour, Manette!" Molly said cheerfully as they kissed cheeks.

Manette shook her head. "Not so *bon*, is it?" she said morosely.

"You're talking about Iris Gault?"

"Of course. She was...she and I were very close."

"I'm so sorry." The two women's eyes met, and got teary. "It's just awful. I had just met her. I definitely wanted to get to know her better."

Manette put some lettuces in a customer's bag and made change. "*Merci, à bientôt*," she said, her voice flat.

"She'd been having a rough time of it lately," Manette said quietly.

"What sort of rough time?"

"Oh, you know. Typical for our age, I guess. She kept saying to me, 'So is this all there is?'"

"Huh. Yeah. That's the big ol' bump in the road, isn't it?"

"Some people seem to sail right over it. But Iris...she was looking for *some*thing, she just—" Manette stopped and put her hands over her eyes.

Molly could see her shoulders shaking as she cried.

"...she just won't have a chance to find it now," Manette finished with some difficulty.

"Was it anything...anything in particular? Job, marriage...or just life?"

Manette looked down the long line of customers. "I can't really get into it now, Molly," she said, gesturing to the people waiting. "Good to see you, as always."

Molly felt chastened. She shouldn't be nosing around this case —she barely knew Iris and had no standing to go around asking a bunch of personal questions when people were grieving. But she couldn't help thinking that surely if Iris *was* murdered...wouldn't they be relieved and gratified if the killer was caught?

Unless, of course, it was Pierre. Molly wasn't sure that would go down well at all, even if he wasn't the most popular man in the village. She couldn't quote the statistics from memory, but in the U.S. at least, women were killed by their husbands more than by anyone else. Was it the same in France?

The Mackleys were leaving and she was never going to deliver their breakfast in time if she didn't get going. Molly hurried out of the Place and down the street to Pâtisserie Bujold, hoping that

Monsieur Nugent would be busy enough to forget his offer to teach her how to make almond croissants.

There was a short line coming out the door onto the sidewalk, more proof of Nugent's talents at pastry-making. Castillac did not attract many tourists but nevertheless the shop had been crowded since the end of June with people Molly had never seen before, some of whom spoke languages she couldn't quite identify, and today was the same.

Monsieur Nugent looked harried behind the counter as he fielded demands from two women pointing and asking him questions, one in Polish and the other in English. He briskly used tongs to pick up croissants and drop them in white paper bags; he rang up orders and took their money, too beset to show his usual appreciation for the female form in all its variety and splendor (as he would describe it).

In fact, thought Molly as she observed from the back of the line, Monsieur Nugent appeared to be on the verge of some sort of breakdown. His face was dead pale and she could see beads of sweat on his brow. His hands on the tongs trembled, as did his voice when he asked who was next. He was not even greeting each customer as she took her turn, which he never, ever failed to do.

Was it the demands of too little sleep and no help? Or was Monsieur Nugent upset about Iris Gault? From the way he was acting one would almost think, Molly thought wryly, that Iris had been *his* wife....

§

DUFORT'S APARTMENT was a spare one-room with kitchenette, the cheapest he could find since his income was much reduced after he quit the gendarmerie. One advantage of the small place, however, was that it took almost no time at all to keep tidy. He got up late on Saturday morning and had the place spick and span within twenty minutes, and decided to have a late breakfast at the

Café de la Place, taking his book on the Napoleonic Wars with him.

"Bonjour, Pascal," said Dufort to the waiter, as he settled at an empty table on the terrace.

Pascal, usually the most ebullient of waiters (and the object of admiration for many of Castillac's women of all ages) mumbled bonjour and stood waiting to hear Dufort's order with a blank expression.

"Is something the matter?" asked Dufort.

Pascal didn't seem to hear. "The usual?" he said finally.

"Yes, the usual. But Pascal—you don't look like yourself. What's wrong?"

"She was so beautiful," he said, shaking his head and walking away, passing right by an empty table with used coffee-cups and plates without putting them on his tray.

Dufort sighed. Yes, Iris had been beautiful, no one would argue otherwise. He wondered whether her beauty had caused her death, directly or indirectly. He wondered...but this was not his case, not his murder. It might not even be a murder at all, he reminded himself, glancing inside the restaurant hoping to see Pascal coming with coffee.

Out of habit from his years as a gendarme he took a quick look around the Place, taking the temperature of the village, looking for any spots of trouble—but the trouble had already taken place, and he could see the effects of the loss of Iris Gault, not only in Pascal but other villagers as well. The market was over and few people were about; the ones that were still around spoke quietly in small groups, which dispersed with hugs followed by wan waves instead of the usual laughter and chatter.

His cell buzzed. It was Florian Nagrand, the coroner. He and Ben weren't close but had enough professional respect for each other that Nagrand was willing to give him a head's up on anything interesting, even after Dufort quit his post.

"Bonjour, Ben," he said in his raspy voice. Ben could almost smell the cigarettes.

"What have you got?"

"I can't say with absolute certainty, but if I had to bet, I'd say she was pushed. No alcohol. Running a tox screen but expect it to be clear."

"Can you give me a percentage?"

"Afraid not. And I won't be able to testify it was murder either —in a situation like this, it's impossible to know for sure unless you saw it happen. But I figured you'd want to know I consider the possibility high, even if it's unprovable from the condition and position of the body."

"I'm grateful, Florian. Thank you."

Florian hung up without saying goodbye. Ben looked again towards the kitchen hoping to see Pascal coming out with his coffee and croissant, but he could see no one, not even Pascal's mother who ran the register.

So Iris Gault *was* murdered. The complicated, unhappy beauty of the village, killed.

Pierre could have done it—can you ever say anyone would never commit murder, no matter what? But I can't believe it's him, Ben thought, at the same time understanding perfectly well that his long friendship with Pierre precluded any objectivity.

Dufort got up and walked into the restaurant. Pascal's mother was hugging her next-door neighbor and crying. Pascal stood with his head bowed, leaning up against a pillar.

"Pascal?" Dufort said gently. "Never mind about the breakfast. I'm going to head out."

Pascal startled and Dufort thought he saw tears in the young man's eyes. Pascal just shook his head, and Dufort went back into the bright sunshine and was considering what to do next when his cell buzzed again.

"You've heard?" said Pierre.

"Yes," said Dufort. "I don't know what to say."

"Say you'll help me."

Dufort took a long inward breath. He felt an unpleasant tingling at the base of his spine that he knew was going to develop into uncomfortable jitteriness, despite having had no coffee. "I'm not sure what I can do," he answered.

"How about figure out who killed my wife? Oh, and keep me out of prison while you're at it. You know they'll come after me," said Pierre.

AS USUAL, Molly scrambled to get back to La Baraque with fresh croissants in time for her guests to have a late breakfast. So far she had been lucky that no one complained about their final breakfast arriving on the tardy side, but everyone was packing and straightening up and doing all those last-minute things that seem to crop up while traveling. Molly went to the cottage first, where the Mackleys were just putting the last bags in their rental car.

"I'm sorry to be so late," said Molly, getting a plate and arranging some croissants on it. "The longer I live here, the more people I know, and the more people I know, the longer it takes me to get through the market."

"It's been an adjustment for us," said Josh. "Back in Chicago, when you go into a store, the less people talk, the better. We want to get in and out as fast as possible, you know?"

"Yes, Boston was the same. Maybe it's just being in big cities? It's just a totally different thing here. All about relationships, not accomplishing a list of chores efficiently."

"I think it's fantastic," said Olive. "I would give anything, literally anything, to be able to move to France for good. Or Italy. Or... well, anywhere, really!"

They all laughed.

"But once we moved, you'd be itchy to move somewhere else," said Josh, reaching for a croissant.

"Yep!" agreed Olive cheerfully.

"So Molly, I hope it's not too personal to talk about, but I got to talking with a guy in a café in the village...."

Molly steeled herself. People talk everywhere, but in Castillac gossip was a major sport, and she worried about what Josh might have heard.

"This guy—his English was shaky but I think I got the gist— he told me you're like the main detective here. That you've solved a bunch of crimes including one that had been cold for years."

"Oh, now," said Molly, feeling terribly pleased and embarrassed. "That cold case wasn't me at all. A kid was the key to that whole thing. Anyway, I don't want you to get the impression that Castillac is a hotbed of crime. It's really so lovely here, and the people are amazing. So friendly and welcoming."

"That's been our experience too," said Olive. "It's been a fantastic vacation. But for me—I think I'd choose someplace bigger, Paris or Bordeaux maybe. The idea that everyone knows everyone, nothing is really private...I don't think I could deal with that."

"She wants to keep her poisoning experiments a secret," Josh deadpanned. Olive raised one eyebrow and Molly laughed.

"Well, it's been wonderful having you and I hope you'll come back for another visit someday," she said, enjoying herself but anxious to get Changeover Day wrapped up so she could get back to thinking about Iris Gault.

After the Mackleys had driven off, she checked her computer to make sure of the names of the incoming guests. Roger Finsterman was staying another week in the pigeonnier, and a Mr. and Mrs. Hale were going to be in the cottage. An older couple from Ohio, that was all Molly knew.

She very much hoped the Hales would be low-maintenance— she had a murder to solve.

Sunday morning at Chez Papa was always slow. No workmen came in for coffee before heading to work. Christophe, the new taxi driver, usually read the paper at the table in the corner while waiting for calls, but he slept in on Sundays. Alphonse, the owner of Chez Papa, wanted to keep the place open as many hours as possible because he believed that sometimes a friendly bistro was exactly what a person needed—whether in a moment of crisis or just everyday loneliness. Any accountant concerned with the bottom line would have told him to open his restaurant only when he was fairly certain of getting enough customers to make a profit, but Alphonse paid no mind to that.

"I'm sorry I have to work again," Nico was saying to his girl-friend Frances, who sat at the bar scribbling on napkins.

"No prob," said Frances, pushing her dark, straight hair behind her ears. "Actually, just shut up for a sec, will you?" She bent over the napkin, which was beginning to shred from her writing on it with some ferocity.

Nico glanced around the bar to see if any chores were left undone, and when he saw nothing, he leaned back, crossed his arms, and watched Frances. When she worked she got so completely immersed in what she was doing that he thought someone could dump a bucket of ice water over her head and she would not stop. He loved her intensity and her drive. He loved....everything about her.

"Okay," she said finally, looking up with a grin. "This jingle is going to make me enough money to take us to the Maldives for a month. You up for a vacation?"

Nico reached across the bar and held her arms, pulling her close enough to kiss. "Anytime," he murmured. "You sure you can take that pale skin to the tropics?"

"There is this invention called sunscreen," said Frances, taking Nico's face in her hands and kissing him on the mouth.

"Is there any moment you are not a wise-ass?" he asked, delighted.

"Not so far," she said, settling back on her stool. "So tell me, what's the deal with Iris Gault?"

"You're gonna be a detective now, too?"

"Nah. Not my thing at all. But I am interested in Iris. I just met her last week. Thought she was interesting. Maybe it's shallow of me, and I know it puts me in the middle of a large crowd—but it's impossible not to be interested in someone that striking."

"Yes. The village beauty." Nico took out a dishtowel and polished some glasses that didn't need polishing.

"I suppose all the men in Castillac were smitten?"

"Pretty much."

"Including you?"

Nico cocked his head, savoring the note of jealousy in her voice. "She was very good-looking, for sure. But not my type."

"And what is your type?" purred Frances.

Nico shrugged. "Women who take me to the Maldives?"

"Not bad," laughed Frances. "Okay but really, what was Iris like? Was she always sort of sad, the way she was last week?"

"I don't know, honestly. I didn't see her around much. I guess she was a serious gardener, so maybe that's where she spent all her time. She came in here only once in a blue moon. Didn't really involve herself in village social occasions, or at least not the ones I go to."

"Hmm, a beautiful hermit. Interesting."

"Are you talking about staying in one of those places where you stay in thatched huts out in the water, with a pier connecting you to the beach?"

"*Oui*, Monsieur. That is exactly what I'm talking about."

"I adore you."

Frances kept her head down, pretending to study the napkin covered with scribbles, as she tried to hide both her smile and the blush that was turning her white skin a rosy shade of pink.

❧

AFTER BREAKFAST ON SUNDAY, Molly met Ben at the Place and they went together to the Gault house to pay their respects to Pierre. It was not the sort of social occasion anyone looks forward to, and without saying so to each other, both of them expected it to be even more difficult since Pierre was not the easiest person to talk to in the best of times.

Which this most certainly was not.

After kissing cheeks in the Place, Ben asked Molly to wait a moment before getting back on her scooter. "I've got something to tell you. Well, two things. First of all..." he leaned close and lowered his voice, "Iris *was* murdered. Not 100%, but probably. Florian says most likely she was pushed down the stairs, which broke her neck."

Molly nodded. "Figured as much."

"You're not a little surprised?"

"Well...no. Should I be?"

"I can't say. *I* was."

"That's because you don't want your childhood friend coming under suspicion, which he immediately will. That's because you always want to believe the best about people. It's part of your charm," she added, grinning at him.

Dufort looked away. "And perhaps the downfall of my career," he muttered. "Well, the second thing is that Pierre's asked me to help. Not informally—he wants to hire me as a private investigator. To find out who did it."

Molly tried to suppress how eager she felt at this news. "And? You're taking the job?"

Dufort pressed his lips together. "I didn't give him an answer. Honestly, I'm not interested in this case. I'm no longer on the Castillac force and I'm not sorry about it. I've known Pierre since we were kids. The last thing I want to do is drive any nails into his coffin."

Molly gave Ben a long look. "So...you think he's hiring you just for cover? You think he killed her?"

He shook his head. "I don't want to think so," he said quietly. "And of course public opinion does not determine guilt or innocence, but I can tell you that people will want to believe he did it, just because his manner can be a little gruff. Pierre's not the back-slapping guy to have a beer with at the end of the day, you know?"

Molly nodded. "But still, he's a talented mason. He works hard. He's lived here his whole life, right? That's got to count for something."

"Oh, it does, for sure. Some of the more objective villagers will give him plenty of credit for that, and for not being the sort to cause trouble. But on the other hand...."

Molly waited. She fidgeted. She raked her fingers through her wild hair and pulled it into a ponytail and secured it with an elastic, and still Ben had not finished his sentence. "On the other hand what?" she burst out at last.

"On the other hand, he married the best-looking woman in the village, possibly even the entire *département*. People couldn't understand it, how a seemingly stolid, dull man like Pierre ended up with her—and what they don't understand they can quickly come to condemn. I think Pierre was largely unsuspecting of how much envy some people felt towards him. Or maybe he just didn't let it bother him. It's not like he was going around sharing his feelings about it."

"Or about anything."

"Right. Close-mouthed as a turtle, Pierre is."

"So you're going to refuse him?"

Dufort shrugged. "I want to. But how can I?"

Molly let out an unintended yip of glee and threw her arms around him. "If he's innocent, he needs you on his side," she said in his ear, a little too loud. "And if he's not—and I say this not because I think he's guilty but because I try to be careful not to assume anything—if he's not, then Iris needs us to bring him to justice. I mean—needs *you*," she corrected, a blush creeping up her neck.

"I don't suppose you'd like to be my second in command?" said Ben, with a slow smile.

Molly beamed. "I'd like to help in any way I can," she said modestly. "But this morning...how about I leave you alone with him for a while, so you can do that *mano a mano* thing."

Ben laughed. "All right. I think you're right that I should speak with him alone first. Hop on your scooter and follow me— the house is right on the edge of the village, it'll take us three minutes to get there from here."

And so just about three minutes later, Molly and Ben parked their scooters and walked up to Pierre's front door.

"That arbor is stunning," said Molly, pointing to a rustic arbor fashioned into a roof, which was covered with wisteria vines. A metal table and chairs was underneath, a perfect shady spot to have morning coffee or lunch.

"Iris was quite a good gardener. Rémy has mentioned she's

won various awards over the years, though I'd never known much about it."

"Gardens aren't really on your radar," said Molly, poking him with her elbow. "What's taking Pierre so long? He's expecting us, right?" She craned her neck to see through the small window in the old wooden door, but could see nothing.

Then they heard the crunch of gravel, and slow footsteps. Pierre appeared from around the side of the house.

Ben and Molly expressed their condolences. Molly hugged him but he did not hug back. Pierre appeared muted, as though perhaps he had just woken up.

"Would you mind if I wandered around the garden?" asked Molly. "I'm sorry to say I only met Iris last week, and only briefly —you remember, at Chez Papa the other night, Pierre? This might sound a little woo-woo but I'd like to pay my respects to her there."

Pierre gestured to the path by way of answering, and then he and Ben went inside.

Awkward, thought Molly, but he has always been awkward. Or not even—it's just that you get the feeling he's more interested in stone-work than people. No crime in that. And grief hardly looks the same in everyone. You can't expect wailing, rage, and loud expressions of anguish just because that's how you'd react if your spouse had been murdered.

And yet...even so, Molly felt uneasy. She had worked with Pierre on the pigeonnier and been more than satisfied with the excellent and artistic job he did. But that did not mean she *liked* him.

Was liking someone even relevant? Couldn't a murderer be likeable, and an innocent man not be?

Molly realized she'd been standing in the path staring into space while she thought. With a jerk she moved forward and forced her attention to Iris's garden. And oh, what a garden it was! Very orderly and geometric, in the French style. A row of parterres containing elegant patterns with neatly clipped low plants. Boxwood hedges around rows of hybrid tea roses. The white gravel paths immaculate, not a weed anywhere to be seen.

Two swan topiaries stood like regal guards over it all, green spirits with neatly defined feathers and graceful necks. How in the world did Iris maintain all of this without help? Or maybe she did have someone, or a fleet of someones, that came in to clip and shape and water and all the myriad chores required for such a high-maintenance endeavor?

Molly was curious about what Ben and Pierre were talking about inside the stone house. But she also felt that she was getting to know Iris a little by staying where she was. A person who made this sort of garden had grand ambitions, that was clear. Was not afraid of work. And, perhaps most interestingly, Molly understood that the design principle was based on control, the effusion of plants held back and not allowed to burst out or run wild even a tiny bit.

On the ground beside one of the swans Molly saw a small scattering of clippings, still green. Was sprucing up the topiary one of the last things Iris had done? Molly imagined her working alone, making the garden exquisite even as her own beauty was just starting to fade. Molly teared up, and knelt down to pick up the clippings and let them fall from her fingers, feeling a wave of sadness at the waste of a life.

Molly's own preference was for gardens with a freer spirit, which favored lushness over rigidity. She could appreciate Iris's garden, but it inspired respect more than joy. And it made her feel a little sorry for Iris Gault, if it was true that the garden was a reflection of her character—if she had lived a life of restraint, and never given herself permission to dance outside the lines.

fter about fifteen minutes, Molly walked to the Gault house, figuring she'd given the men long enough to talk alone. She slipped in through the front door, not wanting to disturb them by knocking. She could hear their muffled voices coming from the back of the house, and she moved quietly down the corridor, stopping to glance in the living room.

It was very, very neat. Scrupulously so. Uncomfortably so. The sofa was an antique, with ornate woodwork but no throw pillows. On either side a small side table. A bookcase filled with books, and not a single one piled on top of the row as was the rule at Molly's house. An armchair with a small round table beside it, three books precisely lined up, and an empty teacup in a saucer. It was spotlessly clean and completely without clutter of any kind.

I'm not exactly a slob, thought Molly, but this house looks entirely too tidy. Do a lot of people live like this? She shuddered slightly. The living room was disagreeable; it felt like it was waiting to rebuke anyone who came in and disturbed it, as though whoever left behind that teacup was going to regret it somehow.

Molly smiled to herself, realizing she'd gotten a little carried away. She stepped back to the corridor and walked closer to the kitchen, wanting to listen to what the men were saying before they knew she was listening. She absolved herself of this misdemeanor by telling herself she would admit it to Ben later on.

"…insurance. I know it looks bad," Pierre was saying.

"Whatever moved you to take out such a large policy?"

"Iris urged me to do it. She could be a little morbid, you know. She would get into these funks and part of it was dwelling on a belief that she wouldn't live into old age."

"Well."

"Yes, well. Obviously she was correct. I suppose I could refuse the pay-out? Or donate it to some cause?"

"I don't think that will matter much," said Dufort. "You might fare better in village opinion, but the gendarmes will look at it as a desperate attempt to throw guilt off yourself."

Molly knocked discreetly on the open kitchen door.

"Come on in," said Ben. "You don't mind, do you, Pierre? Molly has been extremely helpful in past cases, as you might have heard."

"A regular Inspector Maigret," said Pierre, without any hint of a smile.

Molly stood uncomfortably in the doorway. "Do you mind if I ask a few questions?"

Pierre shrugged. He stood up and looked out at the garden.

"I know this is personal, and I wouldn't ask if it wasn't necessary. Maybe you've already covered this? But a crucial thing—how was your marriage, Pierre? Were you and Iris happy together?"

Pierre sighed. "Yes. She was an angel and I adored her."

No one spoke.

"That's what you want to hear, right?" said Pierre, bitterly. "Because when something happens like this, people forget that marriage has ups and downs, rough patches interspersed with happiness, or maybe not even that, maybe the best you get is not miserable—people don't understand how it is. But in their ignorance they will decide my fate."

Ben cocked his head. "That's not correct, Pierre. The evidence will decide your fate."

"Though if part of that evidence is that you loved your wife, that'll help," Molly added quietly.

"We were very happy together. But tell me: how am I supposed to prove that?" asked Pierre.

"No affairs, nothing like that?"

"No. Don't be ridiculous."

Molly bristled at Pierre's defensiveness. She shot Ben a look but he did not meet her glance. "Pierre has a partial alibi," he said to Molly, still not looking at her.

"What's a 'partial' alibi?"

"He was at Chez Papa Friday night. I don't know the time of death as determined by Nagrand, but it would seem as though during much of the window of opportunity for murder, Pierre was —with you, actually."

Molly bristled again. "Excuse me if I'm not understanding, but I thought the idea of alibi implied that you had one or you didn't. If there's any time you can't account for, and it's enough to have committed whatever crime is in question, then...sorry, no alibi. No such thing as a 'partial', in other words."

Pierre glared at her.

"Look, I'm not trying to be difficult. And Pierre, I understand that what I'm saying may not be easy to hear, but what good will beating around the bush do you? Am I missing something, Ben? If, for example, we know that Iris was killed between eight and ten, and Pierre was at Chez Papa from eight until nine, how in the world does that help him at all? To me the facts say he had a nice fat hour that's unaccounted for."

Finally Pierre spoke. "You said that Nagrand didn't confirm the murder, only speculated about it. It might very well have been an accident. So how far do you think the gendarmerie will go with this? Might they poke around a bit and give up?"

Molly and Ben heard the hopeful note in Pierre's voice, and both of them felt a little depressed at the sound.

§☙

THE FOLLOWING MORNING, Molly and Ben met at the Café de la Place for breakfast. A heat wave was gathering strength and even at that semi-early hour it felt more comfortable to sit in the dappled shade of a giant plane tree. They gave their orders to Pascal and affectionately looked at each other across the table.

"You look lovely this morning," he said, noticing how her hair was sticking out crazily on one side.

"Not half bad yourself," she said, grinning.

A few customers sat down at the table next to them—tourists probably, since neither Ben nor Molly recognized them.

"The insurance...that's a bad break," said Ben in a low voice, jiggling his leg under the table.

Molly said, "Hm," and looked out at the Place, which was quiet, with only a few people walking around.

"What's 'hm' mean?"

"Oh, just...."

Ben raised his eyebrows. "You don't trust Pierre."

"No. I don't."

Ben narrowed his eyes slightly as he thought about Molly's answer.

Molly was trying to do what she had found to be the most helpful thing in detective work: not make assumptions. And she certainly wasn't going to assume that Pierre was telling the truth about not murdering his wife, just because he said so. Or because he had been to school with Ben and done an excellent job renovating her pigeonnier.

One thing has nothing to do with the others, in her view.

"He doesn't have an alibi. There's the insurance money for a motive. I'm not saying I definitely think he did it, but you have to admit, it's certainly possible."

Ben finally spoke. "In that case, maybe it's not a great idea for you to be working with me on this."

Molly was nonplussed. "Do investigators always have to believe their clients are innocent?"

"In this case, yes. The job is to exonerate Pierre. Chase down every lead, pursue every avenue that might be productive. I'm going to be doing a lot of interviews, for one thing, and if you're there pulling in the other direction…I think it could be damaging. It could hurt my progress."

"What do you mean, 'pulling in the other direction'? I'm not claiming I know what happened any more than anyone else. I'm not saying I think he's guilty or that I want him to be guilty. Only that I don't necessarily believe Pierre is innocent just because that is what he claims."

"And you think I'm a fool because I do?"

"I didn't say that!"

"It's implied, Molly," said Ben, his expression stony.

They sat for some long moments. Molly was unwilling to budge since she felt she'd only said what made perfect sense to her, and Ben was equally immoveable, feeling insulted.

"I'm going to have a run and get on with it, then," he said, standing up. "You won't mind eating two breakfasts, will you?" And with that, he took off down the street and was out of sight in a matter of moments.

Pascal arrived with two coffees, two freshly-squeezed orange juices, and two croissants, all on separate plates. He looked quizzically at the empty chair.

"Ben had to rush off," said Molly, managing a smile for the handsome server. "But you know me, never let it be said that a cup of good coffee or croissant went to waste on my account!"

She sprinkled a packet of sugar on her café grande and took a good long slurp, closing her eyes, the sweet-bitter-milky flavor sending her into a quick rapture, despite having just had what amounted to her first fight with Ben.

Now what in the world is his problem? wondered Molly, never having known him to get so cranky. And to storm off for no reason? She was irritated with him right back, the way he acted as though she wasn't allowed her own opinions, and thought she was insulting him when she wasn't.

In the case of Pierre and Iris Gault, it was obvious to Molly at least that neither of them knew what had happened. They hadn't even begun to investigate!

Thank heavens her irritation did not get in the way of enjoying her croissant, which she could tell was from Pâtisserie Bujold. There was a signature flavor Monsieur Nugent somehow managed to pull off, an intensity of buttery deliciousness that no other pastry shop could match. After finishing Ben's orange juice, she polished off his croissant, and then decided it was time for a long walk.

It was hot but she had just eaten two breakfasts and she needed the exercise. And she thought that if she walked all over the village, surely she would find some people to talk to who might shed some light on this whole business.

It's not that she set out to prove Ben wrong, exactly. But if that's what happened—at least in the mood she was in in the moment—she wouldn't be all that sorry.

❦ 13 ❦

Dufort started towards the station thinking he would have a word with Maron, but then changed his mind. Sweat was making the back of his shirt damp and he wiped his brow with the back of his hand, though walking a few blocks was hardly any exertion for a man as fit as he was. He cut down a narrow side street and walked away from the center of the village, heading to the herbalist's.

He stopped when her strange little shop came into view. He didn't want to have to go inside. He recoiled at the thought of having to carry around the blue glass vials again, being dependent on the tinctures after being free for so many months.

But it wasn't the treatment that was the real problem. What he didn't want—passionately didn't want—was the tingling up and down his spine starting up again, along with the jangly thoughts, the sweating, the runaway anxiety. He had hoped that when he crossed Valerie Boutillier off the books it would settle things down for good. And he had felt so much better lately, days and even weeks without so much as a prick of worry.

Dufort opened the door to the shop and walked in. The herbalist, a young woman with long tangled hair and no makeup, was leaning on her elbows, on the counter, looking at a large book.

"Bonjour, Benjamin," she said, barely looking up. "Hot today, eh? How have you been?"

He sighed. "Very well, thanks. Extremely well. I haven't used any tinctures in quite some time. No problems at all. But lately, and today...."

"The anxiety is back? Does it feel the same as last time?"

Ben nodded. "I'm not getting the racing thoughts," he said, feeling embarrassed to talk like this to the young woman, and also relieved to share his trouble at the same time. "But the feeling of dread is back. The feeling of electricity in my spine. And I'm jumpy as all hell." He remembered Molly and how he had let a simple disagreement infuriate him. "And I'm suddenly getting really bothered by things that wouldn't have bothered me at all five minutes ago."

The herbalist, whose name was Chloé, looked at Ben with a clinical eye. She asked a long list of questions, some of which sounded very odd to him, but he didn't hesitate to answer them all.

"Now, finally," she said. "What has changed? Are you working a new case, even now that you're retired from the force?"

"Did you know Iris Gault?"

Chloé laughed. "Everyone knew Iris! The goddess of Castillac."

"Just curious...do you have any ideas about what happened?"

"Me? I really can't say, Benjamin. I didn't know her personally, or her husband either. People are saying it was murder, is that right?"

Dufort nodded.

"Well, I'd be looking at the husband then," she said, as she opened a drawer and took out a number of small glass bottles and began adding drops to a larger one. "I mean, it's usually the husband, right? And it happened in their house?"

Dufort nodded again. "Yes, she fell down the back stairs."

"You mean she was pushed."

Dufort nodded reluctantly. He realized that somewhere deep inside he had not really accepted that Iris's death was not an accident. As though the wishful part of himself was thinking that Florian Nagrand would be calling him up any moment to say it was all a mistake, she had just been clumsy, they could all go home and stop looking for a murderer.

"And when you found out that she was pushed, is that when the anxiety ramped up again?"

Dufort was looking at the squiggly pattern on Chloé's dress. It reminded him of studying cells back in biology class years ago—of cell membranes and cilia and all the things living in the world that you need a microscope to see.

"Yes, more or less. Before Iris died—before her husband hired me to investigate—I was doing fine."

"None of my business really. But you might want to think about another line of work?"

Dufort shrugged. "Maybe. It's...it's difficult figuring out what to do, at my age. I thought detective work was what I wanted to do above everything." He raised his palms as though in surrender. "You'd think I'd have sorted it out by now."

Chloé nodded. "Sure, it feels that way. But I see all kinds of people in here who haven't sorted things out, not by a long shot. Maybe it's work, maybe it's relationships, or even just how to manage day-to-day life. You'd be surprised, Benjamin. People struggle. Pretty much everyone, at some point."

"You're kind to say so."

"Now, same as before. Three drops under the tongue if you're having a bad moment, otherwise just five drops in the morning and another five before bed. Come back and see me if it doesn't help."

Dufort thanked her and paid, then headed back to the sunny street. He was thinking about Rémy, who said that everyone has a

NELL GODDIN

mission in life—but easy for him to say when he had a messianic devotion to organic farming.

He preferred to take the drops in privacy, even away from Chloé, and so he ducked into the first alley he came to, looked around, and slid the bottle out of the bag with a sigh. He was going to have to get things figured out this time. He was thirty-five years old. It was time to decide what kind of life he wanted and start living it.

ON HIS WAY to the Monday lunch shift at Chez Papa, Nico took a detour. He left his small apartment over an old stable on rue Pasteur and walked in the opposite direction from the bar, not noticing the hot weather because he was so focused on the purchase he was about to make.

"I've never actually bought flowers for anyone," he admitted to Madame Langevin, after looking around her shop for a few minutes, lost about how to to choose and what to ask for.

"A pox upon you!" she said, glaring at him and then laughing. "Of course that's not a problem, young man. You are Nico Bartolucci, I believe?"

"Oui, Madame," said Nico, unsure what to make of her.

"I am Angela Langevin. Allow me to guide you. You've at least chosen a decent moment to buy your first flowers, although when you come back in a few weeks—and you *will* come back, Monsieur Bartolucci!—the selection will be even more impressive. I have the most amazing bouquets of imported flowers, of course, but the local blooms—just incredible. I've got several new suppliers who just got into the business. A young couple who live way out on rue des Chênes, I thought at first they wouldn't work out at all—they looked so scruffy and unkempt it was hard to imagine they would be able to bring me anything of beauty. But look here—these anemones are from their little farm—magnificent, don't you agree?"

Nico smiled, feeling totally out of his element but not especially minding. "I never knew there was a flower called 'anemone'," he said. "All I know is, well I'm guessing actually—but I think she'd like something that smells good?"

Mme Langevin gave Nico an appraising look. She had been a supporting player in the romances of Castillac for decades, and she could size people up quickly.

Almost too good-looking. Never fallen in love before. Confident, but way down deep, a little fragile. Hell, that describes most of us.

"Can you describe her to me?" she asked, nonchalantly.

Nico grinned. "She's...she's American. Tall and thin, long legs, hair like Cleopatra."

"I meant more her personality, things she likes, so I can have an idea of which flowers might delight her?"

"Oh, right. Well, I...honestly, she's a little indescribable!" he said with a laugh. "She's very direct, says whatever is on her mind. She's musical. Fun-loving. She makes me want to protect her somehow."

Oh, he's got it bad.

"Smell this," said Mme Langevin, wafting a sprig of nicotiana under his nose.

"Wow," said Nico. "Can I have a big bundle of that? I want to make the whole apartment smell that good."

"If your apartment is not big, then yes, you can accomplish that," she said, tearing off a big piece of waxed paper and laying some long stems on it. Then she took a few more branches from the bucket and lay them with the others. "I'll enclose a little card with instructions on how to care for them. They won't last terribly long but that is part of their beauty."

Nico thanked her effusively and walked quickly back to the apartment with the bouquet, hoping that Frances was out so he could get the flowers all arranged and have the apartment perfumed by the time she got home.

It was true, he did have it bad. He was nearly thirty years old, had had plenty of girlfriends but never fallen in love, and now this strange American woman had entered his life, and he could think of absolutely nothing else but pleasing her. But he was finding Frances not all that easy to please, not because she was demanding, but unpredictable, with odd tastes.

But who could resist flowers? According to Madame Langevin, he couldn't miss.

❧ 14 ❧

Perhaps because of the heat, the village was quiet that morning. Molly wandered around aimlessly, hoping to run into anyone she knew, but the streets were practically empty. She went down rue Saterne and saw Madame Luthier's run-down house, its roof collapsing slightly on one side and a pile of trash beside the door. Then over to rue Baudelaire, where old Madame Gervais lived, but when Molly knocked, there was no answer. The lamp store next door was closed, as it always seemed to be, and Molly spent some moments looking in the window, which was freshly organized and displayed several lamps with silk shades that Molly coveted.

The disagreement with Ben...she let that alone. No point picking at it like a scab; she'd just see if they could smooth things over when they saw each other again. In the meantime, she very much wanted to have some news to tell him, some scrap of evidence she'd managed to find. And the truth was—Ben's behavior had stirred her competitive spirit, and she was relishing the thought of presenting him with proof that he was wrong about Pierre.

It made perfect sense—everyone knew that if a wife is

murdered, the husband is the number one suspect. It wasn't prejudice or fairy tales or television shows that made it so: it was statistics. Pulling out her cell, she did some quick googling and found several well-researched articles on the subject of women being murdered in Europe. Chillingly, the statistic for France was six women per month killed by their partners.

Six. Per *month*. It was hardly outlandish to bet that one of them, this July, was Iris Gault.

She walked back toward the Place, drooping from the sun, trying to think of whom she could interview that might have known Iris well. Who might know something, might have heard her talk about Pierre or the state of her marriage?

Right on rue Picasso she found her answer. The primary school was nestled near the center of the village; she had walked by it many times, although the sight of the children running around the playground almost always made her feel melancholy, unable to hold back a flood of regret at not having her own little ones.

But that morning those feelings didn't take hold of her at all—she had a job to do. Molly looked in the windows and saw a man and a woman sitting at their desks. They must have known Iris quite well, she reasoned, and without any hesitation she sailed through the front door.

"Bonjour," she said tentatively, from the office doorway. "Let me introduce myself. I am Molly Sutton. I moved to Castillac about a year ago, from the United States."

"Bonjour Madame Sutton," said the man, springing up from his chair. He was tall and lanky, with longish hair falling over one eye. "I am Tristan Séverin, principal of the school. What can I do for you?" His expression was warm and kind, and Molly felt encouraged.

"Well, I'll just jump right into it. You know Ben Dufort, of course?"

"Oh, yes," said Séverin. "He used to come every year to talk to the students, back when he was Chief. Very entertaining, the children loved him."

Molly smiled. "Well, he's...he's a private investigator now, is that the term? My French is improving but hardly perfect," she said, blushing. "Right now he is looking into the death of Iris Gault. I'm sure Officer Maron has been in to see you?"

The woman, who was still sitting at her desk, dropped something heavy on the floor.

"Not yet," said Séverin. "It's such terrible news. We were very fond of her, weren't we, Caroline? Excuse me, this is Caroline Dubois, my assistant. Couldn't accomplish a thing without her." He smiled at Caroline, who managed an approximation of a smile at Molly but not a very convincing one. Molly noticed that she was well-dressed and quite neat, in contrast to her boss, who looked like he'd just come in from a session on the playground himself.

"Is it true what we've heard?" asked Caroline. "That she was...murdered?"

"I'm afraid that's the coroner's best guess. You have faith in Nagrand's judgment?"

"I've never had any dealings with him one way or another," said Séverin. "I expect he knows his business. But it's very hard to imagine why anyone would want to kill Iris." He glanced at Caroline, who nodded and then looked back at her computer screen.

"Would you have a few moments to talk?" Molly asked Séverin. "I don't want to interrupt your day, but I was walking by and hoped you might have a minute or two now that school is out for the summer. Maybe you could show me where she worked?"

Séverin looked at Caroline. "Nothing pressing?"

"No, it's an easy day, actually. The mailings went out last Friday and you've got an appointment tomorrow morning, but that's all. Besides that mountain on your desk," she added, gesturing with a strained smile.

"Please, deliver me from that mountain," he laughed to Molly, and they left the office together. "So you're working with Ben on this, am I right? You've made quite a reputation for yourself, Madame Sutton, solving crimes left and right! Castillac is lucky to have you."

"Why, thank you," said Molly, the blush deepening. "Yes, I'm working with Ben. He's been hired privately to look into the matter. Though no doubt the gendarmerie is on top of it as well."

Séverin nodded. "Terrible situation. Really—it's unthinkable. Iris was such a gentle soul, I can't imagine how a thing like this could have happened."

"Had she worked at the school long?"

"Yes, for many years. I believe she started out as an assistant cook in the cantine and over time worked her way up to the head position. She came up with the menus, managed the kitchen, all of it really. For my part, it was one area of running the school I never had to worry about—I knew that with Iris in charge, the children's lunch was going to be wholesome, delicious, and served on time."

"So no disagreements, problems with the other workers, anything of that sort?"

"Oh no, not at all." They passed through an empty courtyard and into a very large room in another building. "Occasionally we'd have some back-and-forth about the budget. What chef doesn't want to spend money on the best ingredients, after all?" He smiled. "Sometimes she would get frustrated about that, or about not being able to find enough local vegetables in some seasons. She was very good at her job. Very caring and loving to the children."

"And how did she get on with everyone else? Did the others in the cantine like working with her?"

"Oh yes, certainly, I never heard a word about any problems. You might want to talk to Ada Bellard, her second in command. She'd know better than I would about what went on behind the swinging doors." Séverin gestured at the double doors that led to the kitchen.

"And...I know this sounds terribly nosy, but that's what we have to do...did she ever talk about her husband?"

Séverin started to speak but closed his mouth. Molly had the sensation of wanting to reach down his throat and pull those swallowed words right out. With effort, she kept quiet.

Finally Séverin said, "Well, it doesn't feel quite right to break a confidence. But obviously, this is an extraordinary situation. I have to think about what Iris would have wanted."

"Of course."

"She wasn't one to talk endlessly about her personal problems. But it's true, yes, that things had not been going well with Pierre for some time. I don't know any details. Occasionally she would let slip the odd remark, you understand?"

"I think so." Molly considered pressing him further but did not wish to go too far.

"Marriage is difficult," said Séverin. "I know from experience. My wife—well, I won't bore you with all that. I wish I had more to tell you, but honestly, Iris wasn't airing her dirty laundry in public, even though all of us working here at the school are friends. She was nothing if not discreet." Séverin straightened up and smiled. "Is there anything else? I fear Caroline's wrath if I don't make at least some dent in that pile on my desk."

"I understand, and thank you very much for showing me around. Would you mind if I took a quick look in the kitchen before I go?"

"No, not at all, whatever you like. Hope to see you again, for a less grisly reason. Au revoir, Madame Sutton!"

The principal left the cantine and Molly was alone. The room was cavernous; the lunchtime tables pushed against the wall with chairs upended on top of them. Everything was clean and in order. She pushed open the swinging doors, mindful of this being Iris's place, where she spent so much of her time and energy.

"Oh, excuse me!" said Molly, drawing back.

A man in blue coveralls was hunched over a sink at the end of the kitchen. "Eh, I'll be done in a moment. Something wasn't done right when this drain got put in. It's always clogging up." He emptied a bucket into it, scratched his head, then banged the empty bucket into the bottom of the sink.

"Do you know if Ada Bellard is around somewhere?" asked Molly.

The man said something Molly couldn't understand. He made a short wave before leaving through the back door.

Molly wondered why the drain would be clogged if school was out and no one was using the kitchen. She turned on some more lights and walked through the kitchen, thinking of Iris. Large pots hung from a rack on the ceiling, with many more on wire shelves. Everything was organized, tidy, and sparkling clean: exactly what Molly would expect from Iris given her well-kept garden and house.

The industrial steel counters and stove somehow clashed with her idea of French cooking, and she realized she was romanticizing the whole thing—what, did she think that Iris would be hard at work behind a brocade curtain, cooking for the school in a cast-iron pot over a fire in a medieval fireplace? Just because the food was made from scratch didn't mean the kitchen wasn't modern.

Molly shivered. Even with all the lights on, the kitchen felt dark somehow—or as though something creepy was there and Molly couldn't see what it was. She hurried back through the swinging doors, across the large room, and outside into the heat.

Who *was* Iris Gault? she wondered. Did Pierre kill her in a fit of passion, or did he plan it out? And how much did the insurance money figure into it?

There were a number chores waiting for her at La Baraque. Molly wandered back to her scooter and then zipped home, hurrying through the sweeping up, finishing up some dirty dishes, and deadheading the roses in the front border. She steadfastly refused to think about Ben, or worry that there was anything more than a fleeting irritation between them. And she certainly wasn't planning to hang around waiting to hear from him—tonight she was headed to Chez Papa by herself, and she could barely wait.

❧ 15 ❧

Fortified by the new tincture, Dufort walked quickly to the station. He wanted to meet the new gendarme and talk to Maron about the Gault case. But Maron was not in.

"I'm not sure when he'll be back," said the short man sitting at Therese's old desk. Dufort noticed that his uniform was impeccable and wondered if he actually polished the buttons. "A woman came in about half an hour ago saying her husband was missing again. Maron seemed to know what it was about."

"Ah yes, that would be Madame Vargas. Her husband suffers from dementia, the poor man." Dufort paused, distracted momentarily by thinking about the parts of his old job he had liked, such as getting Monsieur Vargas home safe. Nothing sinister, nothing complicated, and an almost guaranteed happy ending. He shook his head slightly to bring himself back to the present. "I am Benjamin Dufort, formerly Chief gendarme here." Dufort smiled but the other man did not change his expression.

"I have heard of you."

"And your name is...?"

"Excuse me. I am Officer Paul-Henri Monsour. Is there anything I can do for you?"

Dufort understood that Monsour had absolutely no interest in helping him, or having anything at all to do with him for that matter. A Chief who resigns his post—such strange, unaccountable behavior!—is a person to be avoided if at all possible.

Dufort felt that this shying-away on Monsour's part gave himself an advantage, though he couldn't say precisely how. In any case, it amused rather than affronted him.

"Actually, Paul-Henri, I believe you are the man I want to speak to." Dufort knew that using the gendarme's first name would annoy him. "You answered the call to the Gault house on Friday night?"

"I did."

"Tell me what you found, if you please. How was Pierre? Was anyone else at the scene?"

"I am sorry, Monsieur Dufort, but you're asking me to speak about the business of the investigation, and of course that would go against all the protocols of the gendarmerie. Speaking to a *civilian* in such a way, no, I couldn't possibly."

"Of course, I didn't mean on the record," said Dufort.

"Nevertheless."

The two men stared at each other. Eventually Dufort's expression softened. "Just ask Maron to call me when he gets in. Can you do that?"

"My pleasure, Monsieur."

Letting the door bang behind him, Dufort went back outside. It felt as though the temperature had climbed another five degrees and he moved to get under the shade of a oak tree while he considered his next move.

Abruptly he let out a short laugh as he thought how glad he was not to be Chief with Monsour working under him. For a fleeting moment, he imagined what it would be like to leave Castillac, and make a new start somewhere else, where he did not know the histories of most of the inhabitants and felt no responsibility for keeping them all safe.

Then with a sigh he began a list of questions: Did the Gaults socialize with anyone in particular? Who would have insight on their marriage? Who were Iris's confidantes?

And above all, why was Molly so intent on convicting Pierre before they'd even gotten started?

❧

"THANK YOU, NICO," Molly said, wiggling on her stool at Chez Papa and then picking up her kir and taking a long sip. "Good heavens, it was hot today. Have you heard a weather report? When's this heat wave going to be over?"

"I rather like the heat," said Lawrence, sitting on his usual stool with his usual Negroni parked in front of him. "I strip down to a glamorous pair of heathen underwear and bask in my backyard like a lizard."

"You do have an admirable tan."

"I believe my vitamin D status is absolutely tip-top," he said. "So come on, enough about the weather and my skin. How goes it with Iris's case? Is there any hope for poor Pierre?"

"I don't know why you say 'poor Pierre'. He's hired Ben, so he's not exactly defenseless."

"Your eyebrows are knitting. Quite adorable."

"Oh, please. I'm interested in why everyone's so quick to defend him. You must realize that women die at the hands of their husbands and boyfriends more than any other way? For women in their thirties and forties, more die that way than from cancer!"

"That *is* startling."

"I'll say it is. And it makes me angry, Lawrence. It makes me want to slap that damn mason across the face and ask him how dare he hurt his wife, and I don't care two figs about what was wrong in the marriage."

"I agree that being disagreeable shouldn't get you killed. If that's what you're getting at."

"A murderer demonstrates cowardice, lack of self-control, weakness...the list goes on. I admit—and maybe I sound self-righteous—but I have contempt for it. I know that possibly from time to time it can seem as though I'm obsessed with murder, but it's the audacity of the murderer that I can't get past. This idea they have that *their* feelings, *their* hurts, are more important than anyone else's. They are the ones to decide who lives and who dies. It makes me so bloody angry!"

Nico and Lawrence listened warily.

"I don't often see you this upset," said Lawrence. "Perhaps never. Is it really directed all at Pierre?"

"No!" she snapped. "It's also Ben, who's completely on Pierre's side. Willingly taking money in order to defend a wife-killer. What am I supposed to make of that?"

"But Molls, you don't know Pierre did it," said Nico, a little meekly.

"I do too. Statistics may be manipulated, I'll grant you that. But in this case, I think the situation is pretty straightforward. As I just said, women are murdered by their husbands and boyfriends at an alarming rate. Six a month in France—I just looked it up. Six every *month!*

"And the facts are these: Iris was pushed down the stairs in their house. Pierre was there. He made a half-hearted attempt at an alibi by stopping by here, which he almost never does, then called the gendarmes in a weak effort to look innocent. Never has there been a simpler case, it's all laid out plain as day! Are you suggesting, I don't know, that a stranger strolled by their house, ran in, and pushed her down the back-stairs to her kitchen? For what reason, I ask you? Not to mention that statistically, people aren't actually killed by strangers very often. And I haven't even mentioned the fat, juicy life insurance payout. Makes you think, doesn't it?"

Lawrence and Nico exchanged a glance. Molly had jumped off her stool and was waving her hands around, her hair flying out in all directions, her cheeks pink.

"So none of you agree with me?" she said finally, when no one spoke.

"It's you who always says, 'don't assume anything'," said Lawrence.

Molly scrunched up her face. "It's very annoying to have your own words quoted back to you when you're trying to make a point."

"Indeed," said Lawrence.

The door opened behind them and a family came in—a tired-looking mother and two young children, along with a beleaguered father.

"Is the air-conditioning working?" he asked Nico plaintively.

"Sorry, we don't have air-conditioning. You know how it is, Fredo—there's only a few days every summer when we really need it."

"This is one of them."

"Wouldn't argue that point," laughed Nico. "There's a big fan going in the back room. Take your family in there and I'll bring you all some lemonade, how's that?"

Fredo herded them past the bar and into the back room, and Nico got busy cutting lemons.

"All right then, smarty-pants," Molly said to Lawrence. "If Pierre didn't kill Iris, who did? By all accounts she was a gentle woman that everyone liked. Where's any motive for killing her?"

"There's always love."

"Must you speak like a fortune cookie? What do you mean, 'there's always love'?"

Lawrence leaned in close, as though if he kept his voice down, it wouldn't count as gossiping about the dead. "I heard she was having an affair, that's all."

Molly's eyes flew wide open. "*What?* How come no one said anything about this before? With whom?" she demanded, smacking both hands on the bar. "Although before you answer, an affair only strengthens the case against Pierre, you do realize that."

Lawrence shrugged. "Maybe. If he knew."

"*You* know. Why do you think Pierre didn't?"

Lawrence smiled. "Because I know practically everything, my dear. Haven't I convinced you of that yet?"

"Hold on a second. Nico—did you know anything about Iris having an affair?"

Nico shook his head, not making eye contact and continuing to cut lemons.

"You're all completely exasperating!" said Molly, getting back on her stool and drinking her kir, determined to get the name of Iris's lover out of Lawrence if it was the last thing she did on this earth.

❧ 16 ❧

It was Tuesday, the day of Iris Gault's funeral. Molly got up early. She was feeling morose and trying to shake it off. She didn't think she deserved to feel sad—she'd barely met the woman after all. But murder had an effect, not only on Molly but on many in the village: they felt as though no one was safe, not really. It wasn't that they expected Iris's killer to keep on killing, picking off Castillaçois one by one. It was more that if a familiar married couple like Iris and Pierre had argued, and that had led to the fatal shove down the stairs—well, that could happen to anyone, couldn't it? Was everyone just one bad day away from getting offed?

Coffee in hand, Molly halfheartedly wandered around the backyard with Bobo, who did her usual bounding and and flying ahead and then hilariously skidding to change direction, but Molly wasn't paying attention. She turned her head at the sound of a car and Bobo streaked around the side of the house, barking her I-know-you welcoming bark.

I suppose it's Ben, thought Molly, and the corners of her mouth lifted a tiny bit in spite of herself. She stood up straight and followed Bobo, curious to hear if he had any new information to share. She figured she would have to tell him about Iris's affair, but she planned to hold the news back for as long as she could, simply because she was feeling ornery.

Ben and Molly did not say anything at first, but both were sorry about yesterday's spat and it showed in their expressions. They kissed on both cheeks and stood holding hands for a moment, the hot sun beating down on them though it was only eight in the morning.

"Iris was having an affair," Molly blurted out, her orneriness melted by the feel of Ben's hands in hers.

Ben looked startled. "Who did you hear that from?" he asked.

Molly shook her head. "I can't say."

"Lawrence."

Molly shrugged. "So Pierre hasn't said anything to you about it?"

"It might not be true," said Dufort. "I would imagine the rumors about Iris and other men have been bubbling along for years, nothing but fantasies."

"My source is solid."

"Well, even if the entire village believes it, we need to have some proof before racing along whatever avenues an affair seems to open up."

"If you want to get all nit-picky about it, whether it's a rumor or not doesn't actually matter. It's whether Pierre believed she was having an affair—that's what matters."

"Only if you—" Ben closed his mouth and looked down at the ground for a moment. "How about we go inside. You can pour me a cup of your very good and strong coffee. And we can talk this through."

Molly took a deep breath. Why did he have to be so pig-headed? Couldn't he *see?*

Once they were in the shade of the terrace with fresh cups of coffee, Molly said, "All right, there's no point in arguing back and forth until we have more evidence. How can we go about getting that? Who do you think is a likely lover for Iris? Who were their friends?"

"I didn't see them socially. I gather neither of them went out much—Iris was in her garden most of her free time, and Pierre... he works. Always got at least one big project going, sometimes more than that."

"She must have been lonely."

"Possibly. Or maybe she liked spending time by herself. Not everyone is a raging extrovert," he said affectionately, and ruffled her hair. Molly smiled. "It's sort of bad timing with the funeral today, but I plan to ask Pierre to let me search the house. I'll go through Iris's things with this affair idea in mind. Probably Maron has already taken her computer and phone. I doubt he's going to be open-handed about anything he uncovers."

"I wish Thérèse were still here. And it's too bad people don't write letters anymore."

"Yes. A shame for many reasons. I have not written or received any romantic emails, how about you?"

Molly just hooted. "Listen. I don't want to fight with you over this case, Ben. But here's how I see it. Iris was having a kind of midlife crisis. So like—she's hit her forties, and wondering if her life is pretty much done. In her view she's going to keep serving lunch to the kids in the cantine until she's too old to work. She's going to spend all her energy maintaining an incredible garden, because her husband barely speaks to her—"

"—hold on—"

"Let me finish. So, she's not ready to have one foot in the casket yet. She takes a lover. And oh yes! It's amazing to have someone appreciate her! She feels young again! Loved! Except... Pierre finds out. He's furious. They argue, and the next thing you know, Iris is lying at the foot of the stairs with a broken neck. Pierre didn't mean to, not really. It was a heat of the moment kind of thing.

"So what I'm saying is that it wasn't a planned murder, he

didn't do it to get the insurance money or anything like that. A burst of anger, of passion...."

"You could be right."

Molly forced herself not to cheer.

"But I do not believe you are. I know you think that since I have known Pierre all my life that I cannot be objective. And maybe you are correct about that. But it also means that I have an understanding of him that goes quite deep, even though we are not the best of friends and never have been. Proximity for all those years, it adds up to something, Molly."

"Something I will never have."

"Not for Castillac, not for a long while, no. But of course fresh eyes are valuable too, in their way." Ben stretched out his legs and drank some coffee. "You don't have any croissants lying around, do you?"

"Shockingly, no. For once."

"All right, my turn. Here's my version of what happened, off the top of my head with this new information you've gathered about the affair. Let's say you have it all exactly right about the state Iris was in and why she started the affair to begin with. But then something goes wrong. She wants more. She wants her lover to take her away from Castillac, to start a new life in Switzerland, or America...but the lover refuses, for any of a million reasons. Perhaps he only wanted Iris briefly, to prove that he could have the most beautiful woman in the village. Or perhaps he was married, and unable or unwilling to leave his wife.

"They quarrel, and Iris is terribly angry and hurt and she moves to shove him—not to hurt him, only to convey her frustration—and he steps aside, purely out of instinct, and she tumbles downstairs."

"Or...Iris could have broken the affair off, and it was the lover who pushed her."

"That too."

They sat, watching Bobo's speckled head appear and disappear in the tall grass of the meadow, tail wagging like mad.

"We have a lot of work to do," said Ben.

"You're right. Okay, what time is the funeral? Want to go together?"

Ben laughed. "We're probably the only couple in the Dordogne who thinks of a funeral as a really good date."

❧

"MAYBE IT'S INSENSITIVE," Maron was saying to Monsour as they walked up Pierre Gault's driveway the morning of his wife's funeral. "But he's likely to be feeling his loss this morning, of all mornings. We want to see him when his wife's death is hitting him hard."

Monsour nodded. He had never had anything to do with a murder apart from watching them on television dramas, and he was looking forward to making quick work of this guilty husband.

"Not a word out of you," said Maron. "Let me do the talking."

They rapped on the door. Maron felt a trickle of sweat run down under his collar. He wished he'd gotten a haircut recently; he hated feeling damp hair on his neck.

"I don't hear anything."

"I told you, not a word!" Maron cocked his head, listening. From far away, he could hear slow, heavy steps. He imagined Pierre walking downstairs, half-dressed, trying to make himself look as innocent as possible. Maybe even faking some tears.

The door creaked open. "Yes, officers, what can I do for you?"

"We'd like a word. I understand Iris's funeral is today—"

"—in a little over an hour—"

"—which will give us plenty of time. Sorry to bother you on what must be a terrible and sad day for you." Maron looked carefully at Pierre.

Pierre shrugged. "I need about five minutes to finish getting ready, that's all. Whatever you need." He walked into the living room and gestured for the gendarmes to follow.

"I imagine I don't need to tell you that you're in a bad position," started off Maron. His stomach was feeling jumpy and he wished he'd planned out what to say more thoroughly.

Pierre gave a short nod. He did not look concerned.

"So to begin with, if you would tell us your whereabouts on last Friday? The evening of July 11. From nine to eleven."

Pierre sighed. He scratched his forehead. "I'm doing a job, over at the Lafont's. Part I'm on now is a circular staircase made of limestone. It's quite tricky. People don't appreciate the engineering that goes into something like that, with these large blocks of stone needing to be supported as the structure rises up through the air in a column—"

"Yes, I'm sure it's quite complicated," said Maron. "Your whereabouts?"

"I was at the Lafont's until after dark, then dropped by Chez Papa before coming home. I've got some lights set up so I'm not a slave to sunset. I worked on the staircase until around 9, and then neatened up after that. It was dark but I have the lights. Customers are happier if you keep a neat workspace, and I'm a thousand times happier. Can't abide mess."

"And so you left the Lafont's at what time?"

"I didn't look at my watch."

"But sometime after dark."

"That's what I said, yes."

Maron and Monsour couldn't miss that Pierre's annoyance.

"And when at last you got home, what did you find?"

Pierre looked at Maron as though he had two heads. "My wife, lying on the kitchen floor. Is that what you mean? Is this meant to be an interrogation? Because I don't mind telling you, Officer Maron, you're very bad at it." Pierre looked amused.

"Are you not interested in catching your wife's killer, Monsieur Gault?" asked Maron.

"Of course. Which is why your taking up my time with this inanity on the day I have to bury Iris is trying my patience."

"I hear you are a very patient man," said Monsour. "Would you agree with that?

Maron glared at Monsour.

"Stonework requires it," Pierre answered. "Now, if that is all? I'd like to be on time. I'm sure you understand."

Maron and Monsour were ushered back outside into the heat, Maron racking his brain for some other questions to ask, something that would stop this arrogant man in his tracks. The fact that Gault was not falling over himself to help the investigation was very damning in Maron's view.

When he was in Paris, Maron hadn't been afraid of anyone. Now that he was in charge of the small force in Castillac, he was constantly off-balance, his confidence wavering. I'm going to nail Pierre Gault, he said to himself as he and Monsour walked back to the station. I'll prove I don't need Dufort holding my hand to get this guy in handcuffs.

That'll put things right again.

۶.

IT WAS CURIOUS, at least to some.

Iris, whose physical gifts were so extraordinary she should have been whisked off to Hollywood, or at the very least walking the runways of Chanel and splashed on the cover of Vogue, had different ambitions. She simply wanted a houseful of children and a happy family to cook for, and garden to putter in. Some villagers kept hoping she would take off for New York or Los Angeles or Paris and make the village proud, but Iris never showed even a flicker of interest in any of that.

She married the stonemason who doted on her and settled into the house his parents had left him when they died. Everyone who knew her expected pregnancies to come right after. But they did not.

Three years after the wedding, when Iris and Pierre were still quite young and Iris's beauty undiminished, Pierre disappeared on a mysterious errand one Saturday morning. Iris showed only mild curiosity about where he was going and went to the garden to start the day's work.

At Madame Langevin's florist shop, Pierre was not buying flowers but talking to the proprietress, whose old friend in Paris was a friend of a talent scout for a famous modeling agency. Only a few degrees of separation there, it wasn't wrong to use connections when you had them, right? And surely if the desired children were not appearing—for whatever reason—his wife would want to find something else to do. Something that would use her talents to best advantage, thought Pierre. Something that would give her the honor she deserved.

Madame Langevin was happy to help. The friend of a friend came through, and with the agent's name and number in hand, Pierre proceeded to the travel agency and made arrangements for him and Iris to go to Paris for a week. He had never spent so much money before on something so intangible, but it gave him a thrill to be arranging a surprise for his wife, knowing how complimented and encouraged she would feel by his gesture.

"My love!" he exclaimed when he got back to the house and found her still in the garden. A spot of mud darkened her cheek and he noticed that she had thrown off her gloves as she often did, preferring to feel the dirt and plants with her bare hands.

"What is it?" Iris said, unfolding her long legs and standing up with a faint smile.

"I have quite a surprise for you." Pierre put his large hand on her shoulder and squeezed it. He wanted to prolong the moment of anticipation, of imagining her happy reaction.

"Well?" she prodded.

"We're going to Paris in two weeks. I've bought train tickets and made hotel reservations."

"Oh! That's...that's lovely of you," said Iris, her voice dropping. "For how long? We don't want to miss the first roses blooming. I think this year they're really going to come into their own."

Pierre dropped his hand from her shoulder. "Forget the roses for a minute. The trip is only part of it. I've also arranged for you to have a meeting with an agent. He works for Elite, one of the top agencies in the world if Madame Langevin knows anything, and I think she does."

Iris looked up into her husband's eyes. They stared at each other for a long, long moment. Iris felt as though her blood was draining down away from her head, imagining for a split second that it was running right out of the bottoms of her feet and into the ground where she stood.

"I thought I'd explained," she said quietly. "I...I don't want that."

"But Iris! You must know how much—"

"I've told you, being in magazines, all that stuff...it doesn't matter to me. I have no desire at all to leave here. Is money the problem? I've told you, I am more than happy to work. I would be glad to get a job here in Castillac."

"No!" Pierre shouted. "It's not money! Money is not the point at all!"

Iris stepped back. She looked down at the tender rose leaves just unfurling from a Comte de Chambord. She raised her eyes once more, hoping to see some softness in her husband's expression, or at least a willingness to understand what she had tried to explain to him so many times. She did not like being the center of attention; all she wanted was babies, and failing that, to work in her garden.

But Pierre was glowering at the Comte de Chambord and he reached out and tore off a fresh green shoot loaded with tiny buds, then threw it on the garden path and stomped on it.

Iris walked rapidly around the side of the house, picking up a pair of gardening shears on the way, and busied herself with pruning the wisteria in the front arbor while tears spilled down her cheeks. Pierre stood in the garden utterly baffled, tiny rivulets of blood marking where the rose thorns had torn up his hand.

❦ 17 ❦

The last funeral Molly had gone to was the one for Joséphine Desrosiers the previous fall. It had been raining a little, and there had only been a handful of mourners present (if you could even call them that, Joséphine not being known for her warmth and generosity.) The Gault ceremony was shaping up to be an entirely different thing; as Molly and Ben walked down rue des Chênes to the small village cemetery, they could see a long line of cars parked, reaching almost all the way to the village. A crowd stood by the iron gate and another throng was inside. It looked as though every single resident of Castillac was in attendance.

"I don't see Pierre, do you?" Ben murmured, taking Molly's hand.

Molly squeezed his hand and shook her head. "The whole world is here! She must have been very popular."

"Or admired. Not really the same, is it."

"When you're young, being admired seems like exactly what you want. But it's really not worth that much, I don't think. Nothing compared to having real friends."

Ben nodded. He was scanning the crowd and nodding at people he knew. "Madame Bonnay," he said. "Is Yves well?"

"Very well," answered Madame Bonnay. "But this—it is wrong for us to be at Iris's funeral. She was taken too young, too young indeed!"

Ben nodded and pulled Molly behind a mausoleum. "If she *was* having an affair," he whispered, "then he'll be here, almost certainly."

Molly nodded. "Let's split up. We'll be able to watch more people that way."

So Ben went left, towards Joséphine Desrosiers's grave, and Molly went right, towards a brother and sister she hadn't seen in a few months.

"Michel! Adèle! Hello! You're back in town?"

Adèle, looking more fashionably dressed than ever and with a stunning handbag on her arm, kissed cheeks with Molly and then hugged her. "Just passing through really, have some paperwork to deal with. Oh, it's so good to see you!"

"You too. I have to say, having some money sure seems to agree with the two of you."

"Ha!" said Michel. "I think it would agree with anyone. Listen Molls, we're buying a house in Provence, and you absolutely have to come visit. Promise you will?"

"Of course I will! Oh, that sounds dreamy. Now...I don't mean to hurry off, but I'm..."

"She's working a case, Michel," said Adèle. "See that furrowed brow? The way she's running her eyes over the crowd, searching? I know the signs."

"No points for figuring that out, sis. Everyone knows Iris was murdered."

Molly looked towards the street to make sure the hearse hadn't yet arrived. It was rude to be chattering away right there at graveside, but on the other hand, who was she going to offend?

Not Iris, sadly enough. And she didn't much care what Pierre thought.

"Okay listen, before I rush off—tell me what you know about Pierre and Iris. Happy couple? Not? Do you know anyone who used to hang out with them?"

"That's a lot of questions," said Michel, shaking his head. "All I know is that when Iris was younger, the whole village was in love with her. She had these incredible eyes, it was like looking into sparkling water..."

"Michel had a crush on her," said Adèle. "She was older, and completely unattainable. Nobody could believe it when she married Pierre."

"How come?"

"Well, you know him, right? He's not exactly Mr. Excitement."

"Some people don't want that in a partner. They want stability, predictability...."

Adèle shrugged. "The thing is, Iris could have had anyone. You met her? I'm sure she was still attractive, in her forties. But when she was young? Traffic would literally stop. She was a *goddess*. Marrying a mason who only wants to talk about stones just didn't seem like the best use of her options."

"Maybe he really loved her," said Michel.

Adèle shrugged again. "What is love, anyway? I can imagine at a certain point being that beautiful would get tiresome. It's not like your looks have anything to do with who you are, not really. It's not an accomplishment or something you worked hard to achieve, you know? Just luck."

"Not that we're taking a stand against luck," laughed Michel, "since we got a big walloping serving of it ourselves."

"True!" said Adèle. "You're unnaturally quiet, Molly, what's up?"

Molly used both hands to lift her damp hair off her neck in the hope that the slight breeze would cool her down. "I'm listening. And thinking about what you're saying. All right, I do need to go. So lovely to see you both. Call me about visiting Provence, I'll show up at the drop of a hat!"

People were pressing in on every side and there wasn't much room to turn around, but she managed it without knocking into anyone too dramatically. She tried to get closer to the grave but there was no room. Finally she walked away from the mob and up a small slope, where she could see every well, if at a distance.

Pierre stood by the grave. He appeared to be looking into the hole, his big hands dangling by his sides, the sleeves of his coat a little too short. He looked stoic. Stony.

Behind Pierre a man was crying, his face covered with his hands. Molly watched him, wondering who he was. She could hear more sniffling, by men and women, and as the pall-bearers entered the cemetery with the coffin on their shoulders, the crying got louder.

The man behind Pierre dropped his hands, his eyes on the casket. It was Pascal.

Did he have a crush on Iris too? Or was it more than that?

She felt iron fingers close around her arm. "Molly!" gasped Nugent. His face was contorted and she could see actual tracks of tears on his cheeks.

"Monsieur Nugent," she said gently. "I'm so sorry." She couldn't help being moved by his raw emotion.

"Did you know her? She was...she was perfection, Molly. I...."

Molly waited, but Monsieur Nugent had bent his head and dissolved into tears. She was pretty sure she had never seen so many men crying in one place. Did men in France cry more easily, or had Iris cast a spell over the menfolk of the entire village of Castillac?

The priest in black robes was beginning the service. Molly murmured an excuse to the pastry chef and had to pry his fingers from her arm; she moved a few more steps up the slope in order to see better.

There was Caroline Dubois, her face waxen, shoulders drooping. Next to her was Tristan Séverin, also blinking back tears, his arm around a nicely-dressed woman who stared at the ground. Behind them was Manette and her husband, Molly's neighbor Madame Sabourin, and Alphonse from Chez Papa. All of them looking sorrowful, and many dabbing at their eyes with handkerchiefs.

She kept returning to Pierre, observing him. He seemed so alone despite being in the center of such a crowd. People spoke to him but he received no hugs, no reassuring arms around his shoulders. He didn't even look particularly sad. Come *on*, thought Molly. It's your wife's funeral! Can't you even pretend to feel a little upset?

Maron was there, just behind Pierre, and Molly saw a short man in uniform next to him, Therese's replacement. She wondered who they thought had killed Iris, or whether they had any possible explanations for the murder at this point. She moved a few steps to the side so she could see another set of faces. Everyone's eyes were pinned to the casket, which had a frankly magnificent coverlet of flowers—the florist had really outdone herself.

Which, blessedly, gave Molly the best idea she'd had in days.

❦ 18 ❧

The next day Molly puttered around La Baraque for a few hours after getting up and having coffee. She checked on the Hales, who were indeed the lowest maintenance guests possible—they were introverted and capable, and managed the details of their vacation without any of Molly's help. She'd had to curb her instinct for chatter once she saw that the Hales weren't interested in small talk, but it was a relief to know they were getting on fine without her guidance or attention. Roger Finsterman had already taken off, probably somewhere hard at work with his easel and palette.

By ten o'clock she guessed the florist shop was open, and rode her scooter into the village, the breeze feeling wonderful since the heat wave showed no signs of relenting.

The shop didn't look like much from the outside. The window was fogged up and there was nothing on display outside, which made sense given the heat. Molly went inside to the tinkle of a bell, grateful to feel real air conditioning which was not common in the village.

"Bonjour, you are the famous Madame Langevin?" said Molly,

barely able to tear her eyes away from the incredible blossoms in rows of shiny steel buckets.

"*Oui*," the older woman said. "And I believe *you* are the famous Madame Sutton, the detective celebrated by all of Castillac?"

Molly looked at her sharply, thinking she was being sarcastic. But Madame Langevin opened her arms and smiled. "I am teasing you a little," she said. "We are very grateful for what you have done. I am friends with the mother of Valerie Boutillier," she added, referring to an earlier case. "So tell me, what can I do for you? Would you like me to make some special bouquets for your guests at the gîtes? This time of year I could do it very reasonably, and of course nothing makes one feel more special than a bouquet."

"I thoroughly agree. In fact, that is the reason I came to see you today, though not for the gîtes. I saw the flowers you did for Iris Gault's casket yesterday—"

Madame Langevin shook her head slowly. "A terrible business."

"Yes. It sure is. Did you know her?"

Madame Langevin paused, just briefly. "I did. Not very well—she wasn't what you would call a sociable person, to be honest. I don't mean that she was unpleasant or anything like that. Just liked to keep her own company. A very talented gardener—I used to ask her every so often if she would consider growing some special things for me, it could have been lucrative for both of us. She wasn't interested."

Molly knew Madame Langevin was not likely to want to tell her what she wanted to know, and her mind was running around in circles trying to think of something to say which would convince the florist to talk. She reached out to some roses and rubbed a glossy leaf between her fingers, then raked her hair behind one ear, thinking.

"Well, I'll just be direct with you. I don't suppose it would be a big surprise to hear that I'm trying to find out what I can about Iris's murder?"

Madame Langevin nodded, with a small smile. "I don't think I'm going to be much help there."

"What I'm wondering—and believe me, I know this is unforgiveably nosy—but you understand I'm asking because I'm looking for the truth, not to gossip or stir up drama. And it occurred to me that you, out of anyone in Castillac, might have particular knowledge of the romantic goings-ons in the village. The ones behind the scenes, I mean."

"You mean who's having affairs? And with whom?" Madame Langevin laughed loudly, then walked over and checked one of the buckets to make sure it had enough water. "Well, that's rather clever of you. I do know...a few things here and there...though of course, sadly, not everyone who is involved in an amorous liaison sends flowers. They absolutely should, you know. And you might be interested to know that these days, women send flowers to men more often that you'd think."

"What I'd be *very* interested to know," said Molly, moving closer to the other woman, "is whether any flowers were going to Iris Gault. Or being sent by her, as you say. Of course she was an amazing gardener, but if she was interested in secrecy she might have done her flower-sending through you?"

Madame Langevin looked away. Molly could tell she knew something.

"I know she was having an affair," Molly said. "What I don't know...is with whom?"

Madame Langevin kept walking away from Molly. She did not answer at first. Finally she plucked a white rose from one of the metal buckets. "Do you know the symbolism of roses, Madame Sutton?"

"Please, call me Molly. Red for love? That's about all I know."

"White is purity, as you might guess. Also—secrecy, and silence." She pinched a wilted leaf and put the white rose back with the others. "I'm sorry, but I cannot in good conscience give you the information you seek. I...well, I can't honestly say that I am sorry, because I view myself as performing a valuable service to the village, and while part of that is knowledge of flowers, arranging and choosing the most appropriate blooms et cetera— another part is my discretion.

"My customers know that they can ask me to send flowers to whomever they like, and I will never betray their confidences. If I did, what a frosty pall would fall over the village! And I would go out of business," she laughed, but mirthlessly.

Molly studied the other woman for a moment. She was glamorous, in a modest sort of way: her skin well-cared-for, her hair swept back in a dramatic up-do and carefully dyed, her makeup perfect and not overdone. For a moment Molly wondered about Madame Langevin's amorous liaisons, as she'd put it, but then she brought her attention back to Iris Gault.

"But you must see, we could be talking about the person who killed her," said Molly.

Madame Langevin waved her hand. "Oh, perhaps, perhaps. I heard it wasn't definitely murder anyway. People do trip and fall, you know."

Molly did know. She had fallen flat on her face just the other day, when she wasn't looking where she was going and tripped on a shovel. But there was not one thing about this case that made her believe that was what happened to Iris. Maybe that was depending too much on intuition, she couldn't say. Maybe that's where the investigation would end up, with nothing but dead ends, and no conclusion to draw other than the poor woman had suffered a tragic accident.

But Molly wasn't there yet, not by a long shot.

THE SCOOTER MADE a worrisome new noise on the way back to La Baraque. It went along with its usual putt-putt-putt, and then every so often a faint screech interrupted the rhythm. Molly's gîte business was sturdy, and she had bookings right through to September, but with her grand plans for expansion, her budget was still vulnerable to any unexpected expense.

Maybe it just has a slight cough. It'll pass.

She parked it by her front door and knelt down to receive Bobo's frantic welcome. Her tail going like mad, kissing Molly's face, letting out a few strangled yips—yes, a dog's love really is the best. Unlikely to push you down the back stairs, she thought darkly, feeling annoyed because she hadn't been able to figure out a way to get Madame Langevin to talk.

But surely the florist wasn't the only person in town who had eyes. Wasn't Castillac known for being a population of out-of-control busybodies? Getting a name was simply a matter of asking the right person.

Molly thought back to the funeral and all those weeping men. One of them had probably been Iris's lover. One of them was probably Iris's killer. And whether that person was one and the same...no idea.

She pulled out her cell and made a call before she could talk herself out of it. (And was she the only person in the village to have Pâtisserie Bujold on speed dial?)

"Âllo?"

"Monsieur Nugent?" she said tentatively.

A short silence. "Is this Madame Sutton?" he asked. "I have told you, the morning is better to get your croissants, if you require a specific kind. By now it is after lunch, and much of my stock has been sold."

Molly was disconcerted at his brusqueness. He usually seemed so thrilled to hear from her. "I'm actually not calling about pastry," she said. "Well, I mean, not about buying them anyway. You mentioned, maybe last week, that you would be willing to give me a few lessons, so I could try to make my own occasionally? Is that offer still good?"

Again, a short silence. Molly had thought he would jump at the idea.

"Yes, Madame," he said. "If you would like, you can come this evening, before dinnertime. Would six o'clock be suitable?"

"Yes! That sounds perfect. I'm looking forward to it!" Molly thanked him effusively and made her goodbyes. But why had he sounded so dutiful and unenthusiastic? After ogling her practically every day since she moved to Castillac, she had thought he would be hot to trot about the idea of being alone with her on the same side of the counter, for once.

People are never-ending mysteries, she thought, going inside to make a late lunch out of whatever delicious odds and ends she could find, and promising Bobo a treat.

19

N ico and Frances were enjoying a rare day off, deciding ahead of time to dedicate the entire day to doing absolutely nothing they were supposed to. No chores, no work, nothing but whatever struck their fancy at the moment, in keeping with Franny's intention to concentrate on fun for the rest of the summer.

The first bump in the road appeared early, when it became clear that Nico and Frances fancied different things. But they sailed over that by taking turns. They did a round of rock-paper-scissors to see who went first, which Nico won, and were ensconced in armchairs playing a video game when the doorbell rang.

"You answer it," said Nico, unwilling to let his wizard quit the battle being waged to save the world from destruction.

"Happily," she said, putting down the controls. She opened the door to Madame Langevin's deliveryman, holding a gigantic bouquet of red roses.

"Nico!" she shouted.

He peered quickly around and grinned. "Bonjour, thanks for stopping by." And then he went back to his wizard.

"Are you leaving me to tip for my own flowers?" said Frances, laughing.

"We don't really do that here," said Nico as he jabbed at a button on the controls. "Merci," said Frances, using one of her only French words, and the deliveryman grinned and took off.

"They are spectacular," she said, burying her nose in them. "No smell. But their looks make up for it. Every single one is perfect," she said, caressing the blossoms gently with her fingertips. Molly had taught her how to care for fresh flowers, and she took them to the kitchenette and chopped off the stems, then put the blooms in a vase with water.

"Nico...." she said.

"I'm about to kill this shaman," he said, his eyes still on the game.

"Nico," she said, with some urgency, and then collapsed on the floor with her eyes closed.

❧

"I'M JUST GOING to learn how to make pastry. Don't worry about me," Molly said while stroking Bobo's ears. "And don't look at me like that," she said to the orange cat, who was glowering from her perch on the back of the sofa. "I know perfectly well you don't care whether I live or die, so you're not fooling anyone. I'll give you some cream when I get back."

She glanced past the meadow to the pigeonnier, but there was no sign of Finsterman, and all was quiet at the cottage. So, anxious to be on time, Molly hopped on the scooter (still suffering from a dry cough) and sped to Pâtisserie Bujold for her first lesson with Monsieur Nugent.

"Glorious to see you," he said with a wide smile when she came in the shop. "You're right on time. I do admire punctuality. Now then, I've given this enterprise some thought. I'm going to do my best to refrain from lecturing you: you already know my opinion about the futility of attempting to learn quickly an art that takes many years to master." Nugent looked around for something to straighten but everything was already put away and shipshape. "I'm not at all sure you have the required persistence, Madame Sutton, though I will grant that you do have the necessary love for pastry. No one could say you lack *that*." His gaze, as usual, lingered on her chest. Molly had worn a modest shirt, buttoned up to her neck, and she wondered why she had bothered. It was probably going to be scorching, working around these big ovens.

"First of all," he said, handing Molly an apron, "this project we are embarking on...I warn you, it is intimate. You cannot make good pastry only with the mind and the hands. It takes emotion; it takes *feelings*."

Molly swallowed hard. She nodded, backing up a step.

"I hope you don't think it impertinent if I suggest we *tutoyer*, as well as call each other by our first names? I am Edmond," he said, with a little bow.

"That's fine," said Molly, wanting to jump straight to prodding Edmond for village gossip, but finding some stray shred of self-control. "So, what's the first step?"

"Oh Molly, I knew this about you. You *rush*. You are chronically in a *hurry*. And this...this is not good for pastry. I ask you, before we begin—do you have the capacity to go slowly? To allow me to guide you, my dear, down the paths we must follow, consciously, deliberately, in the making of this paragon of French cuisine?

I would rather be digging for maggoty corpses in a swamp with my bare hands.

But she thought of Iris and answered "Yes, Edmond, I can do that. Lead on!"

Painstakingly he showed Molly how to measure and sift the flour, then mix the dough. With an extravagance of verbiage he talked about the importance of spreading the cold butter over the rectangle of dough and folding it, and then again, and again. He interjected bits of history as he went along, telling her that the predecessor of the croissant first appeared in the 14th century in Austria, how the crescent shape might have been inspired by the crescent on the Turkish flag, about the effects of sugar prices and Marie Antoinette.

Molly found the history and the work sort of hypnotizing. It was very involved, quite physical and with many steps, so that she forgot all about the end result and only focused on what they were doing at that moment, and then preparing for the next step. Everything in the correct order, because that was the only way to get the bubbles of air to rise when the dough was baked.

"Of course we are making a plain croissant today, but making the almond version is not difficult once you understand the basic method," Nugent was saying.

"Is everyone in the village your customer?" Molly asked, looking for a way to get Iris into the conversation.

Nugent laughed. "Not everyone," he admitted. "But quite possibly the laggards have some family connection to some of my competitors, and don't want to risk hurt feelings. Or they simply have not come in and sampled what I can do, and so are making their choices without basing them on any actual evidence."

"Are the Gaults your customers?" She knew the transition was awkward, and probably transparent, but she was out of patience.

Nugent stiffened. He clamped his teeth together and turned to Molly with an expression of anguish. "I would prefer to avoid that subject," he said, squatting down and pretending to look for something on a low shelf.

But Molly pressed on, tossing out what she hoped was an irresistible bit of bait. "I wondered, because I heard a rumor, and I have no idea whether it is true or not. And I just thought, well, who sees more villagers than Edmond, day in and day out? Perhaps some of them confide in you? Or maybe you notice things, I don't know—like something between two people, that they think they're hiding but actually they're not doing a great job of it."

"I know my customers better than they know themselves, in some cases. They confide in me, oh yes, but they do not realize they are doing so. I know when they are upset, when life has thrown difficulties their way. When someone has eaten palmiers for years and suddenly switches to a pistachio tart? Oh, it means something, Molly, it means something."

"I meant...more like you probably overhear conversations sometimes."

"That too," said Nugent, drawing himself up.

"And maybe when people are excited—or in love—they want to splurge? Maybe they order a big cake or a fancy tart when they normally don't?"

"Indeed," said Nugent, handing Molly a large ceramic bowl.

"So you might see that, if two people came in—that they were in love? Or maybe even...just lust?"

Nugent stood up, his eyes flashing. "I did not notice anything of the kind! And for her to choose that...that *man-boy!* It's unconscionable. It's beyond the beyond!"

Ah, here we go. The fish took the bait, now I just have to reel him in.

"I didn't know Iris well," said Molly carefully. "But I was surprised too. Wouldn't have guessed it."

"People have affairs all the time," said Nugent, waving his floury hand. "It is part of life, the spice! It is her choice that shocks one."

"Yes," said Molly. She held her breath, praying Nugent would keep talking.

"She made a terrible mistake, choosing that ridiculous Tristan Séverin," he said, his teeth still clamped together.

Bingo!

"I had thought she was the most beautiful woman I had ever seen, though of course no competition for you, Madame Sutton.

But when I heard about Séverin, I admit, I lost some respect for her. We are defined by our choices, you know."

Molly nodded, her mind racing, already formulating a narrative in which Iris broke it off with Séverin and he killed her in a fit of rage. He had seemed to be a decent sort of man, mild-mannered even, but Molly believed nearly everyone was capable of murder if the right button was pushed, and maybe losing Iris had been Séverin's.

Or, of course, it could be Pierre, acting in a fury of jealousy. Either way, the affair was the key to what happened, and she had it safely in her pocket.

"What are you doing?" shrieked Nugent. "Molly, you cannot press the dough so roughly or the butter is going to poke through and all will be lost!"

Molly gasped. "So sorry, I got distracted for a moment. Are we nearly done?"

"You're so very impatient, my dear. I am trying to impart to you that making pastry is like long, slow lovemaking—you cannot rush it! You must, above all, *respect* the dough."

She sighed to herself. Even if she was stuck with Edmond for several more hours, the venture would be totally worth it. She had the name of Iris's lover, and felt confident Pierre was going to be in for some pointed questioning. An arrest might not be right around the corner, but there was progress.

Baby steps. But baby steps were a whole lot better than nothing.

20

S he wasn't proud of it, but Molly didn't call Ben right away to tell him the name of Iris's lover. She was enjoying having the information all to herself, just for a few hours: turning it over in her mind, imagining how the affair started, wondering who else in the village knew. And did the affair give Iris what she was looking for, Molly wondered. Her own marriage had slammed against the rocks when her husband had an affair, but once she peeled off the top layer of hurt and humiliation, she had understood that the cheating was more a symptom than a cause.

Although she was wary of applying her American viewpoint to something the French felt quite differently about.

And what about Madame Séverin? Was she just an afterthought, if that? Or was her health and mood so poor and intractable that you could understand her husband wanting to find love somewhere else? So many questions, and such a complicated yet common situation....

The following morning, after her first cup of coffee, she called Ben and asked him to come over, and then she waited on the terrace, feeling the heat rising. Bobo was flopped in the shade, taking a nap.

In less than fifteen minutes she heard Ben's car turn into the driveway and Bobo roused herself to trot around the side of the house to greet him. Molly was very glad to see him. After they kissed cheeks she pulled him into a hug and held him there for a long moment, appreciating his solid, trustworthy self.

"Well bonjour to you," he said with a grin. "Okay, what did you find out?"

"How do you know I found out something?"

"I think the English expression is, the cat who ate the bird?"

"The canary," laughed Molly. "Well, okay Sherlock, I *do* know something. Want to play Twenty Questions? Who was Iris Gault's lover?"

"I do not want to play. Tell me."

"Tristan Séverin."

Ben nodded his head slowly. "Who told you that?"

"Nugent, of all people."

"Yes. I can see it, I suppose. Although you understand that at this point, all you have is rumor? Just because Nugent said it—that's hearsay, not evidence."

"The world runs on hearsay," countered Molly. "Once it becomes common knowledge, will all the men in the village despise Séverin as well as Pierre?"

Ben shrugged. "I don't think so, no. Of course Iris was still very beautiful, and you know French men do not only admire twenty-year-olds." He waggled his eyebrows at Molly. "But an affair...it is not the same as marrying her when she was still young, you understand?"

"Not as much like driving your flag into the conquered territory?"

"A violent and not very charitable image, *chérie*. Tristan, he is much beloved by the parents of the village. I never heard a word against his running of the school. And not an easy job, either."

"I'm sure it's not. I liked him, and his assistant too. Want some coffee? I even have some stale croissants if you're hungry."

"Ones that you made? How did the lesson go, apart from prying information out of the poor man?"

"It was never-ending...but worth it. I think I could make a decent croissant, with practice. And Nugent spilled the beans easily once I put a little pressure on. He's very upset about Iris. I suppose it's no surprise he's one of the legion who had a huge crush on her."

Ben poured himself some coffee and looked out at the meadow, thinking.

"So the obvious conclusion is that Pierre killed her out of jealousy, or maybe—but less likely—Séverin did it during a lover's quarrel," said Molly.

"I thought Pierre did it for the insurance money," said Ben with an edge of sarcasm.

"No rule that you can't have two motives."

"How about Nugent? He could have done it out of anger, because when Iris eventually took a lover, she didn't choose him," said Ben.

Molly's eyes widened. "I know you're joking. But...it's actually plausible...."

"How about you go have a talk with Caroline? If a boss is having an affair, the assistant will surely know. Maybe she has some insight into his state of mind lately."

"I'm on it!" She was thrilled to have an assignment, and grateful that Ben apparently seemed to think Caroline would be more likely to open up to her than to the former chief of gendarmes. "Okay, so, I know I asked you to come over, but I'd like to run a comb through this bird's nest on my head and then get to it. There's not a moment to be lost!"

WITHOUT CONSCIOUSLY THINKING ABOUT IT, Molly dressed according to Caroline's style before going to find her. She wore a charcoal pencil skirt she hadn't put on since she left Boston, a tailored blouse, even spiffier underwear. The skirt was something of a challenge on the scooter, but she hitched it up and made it work. A half hour after saying goodbye to Ben, she was pulling into the spacious parking area in front of the school and could see Caroline at work in the school office.

Luckily she did not see Séverin. He could just have stepped out for a moment, thought Molly, hurrying to get inside and talk to Caroline before he reappeared.

"Bonjour, Caroline!" Molly said, knocking on the open door as she spoke.

"Ah! You startled me. Bonjour, Molly, how are you?"

"All fine. If a little warm." She fanned her overheated face and smiled. "I was wondering if you have a minute to talk? I just have a couple of questions. It would be immensely helpful if you could."

A lot of people light up when you ask them if they can talk. They like the interaction, the social contact, and of course, almost everyone likes to talk about herself.

Apparently not Caroline.

First she hesitated, then shuffled some papers on her desk as though they were so important she couldn't pause even for a second. Then she straightened her already straight posture and said, "Yes! Of course. Anything at all. Would you mind if we walk at the same time? I get sick of being inside all day just sitting at a desk."

"Sure," said Molly, wondering why Caroline was nervous. They chatted about the weather and which vegetables had been in season at the market last week. They passed the *mairie*, a pâtis-serie Molly had never tried, a mother with her toddler. Finally Molly said, "Listen, I'll just come right out with it. I've had information about something and I'm looking for corroboration, that's all."

Caroline didn't say anything.

"Monsieur Séverin. You've worked with him for a long while?"

"Not so very long. Three years, about."

"You like him? He's decent to work for? Believe me, I've had some horror shows for bosses so if he's difficult, I get what that's like. And please understand, I will not go back to him with anything you say. This is a confidential conversation."

Caroline nodded. "Um, yes, we get along all right. We're well-matched, actually. He's the brilliant, all-over-the-place outgoing type, and I'm very organized. I make sure the forms get in on time," she added with a tight smile.

Molly nodded. "I understand. And...I hope this doesn't make you uncomfortable, but I need to ask about...his private life. I understand his marriage...."

"Well, his wife is ill, that's no secret. Depression. She refuses any kind of help and it's been understandably difficult for Tri—Monsieur Séverin."

"Right. Totally home-bound, is what I heard?"

"Agoraphobic, among other things. Terrified to leave the house."

They walked on, crossing the street to be in the shade. "And...do you have any knowledge of an affair? Either currently or earlier?"

Caroline shook her head. "No, nothing like that. I wouldn't say he's been Mother Teresa about his situation, he gets frustrated as anyone would, but on the whole I think he's been good to his wife. He does what he can, even though she won't let him do very much."

Molly was taken aback. She had been coasting along, expecting to cross confirmation of the affair off her list.

"You're sure about that? Do you think it's possible he could have an affair and hide it from you?"

Caroline laughed. "I don't think you understand the degree of his disorganization. He would need me to keep track of when and where he was meeting her!"

Molly laughed genuinely at that, feeling mystified. Did Nugent have the wrong man? And how had Nugent come by the information, anyway?

21

Ben took off before lunch and Molly had chores around the house she wanted to avoid. Frances was always good for help in procrastinating so Molly called but got no answer. She ate a nice lunch of cheese, pâté, and salad with a refreshing glass of rosé. She lay down on the grass in the backyard and petted Bobo until the dog had had enough and wandered off in search of some quiet shade.

It was hot. Too hot to work in the garden or do anything outside.

Molly caught up on her email, making sure her calendar had all the upcoming bookings correctly marked. She was just about to go ahead and clean the bathrooms and look at that soft spot in the floor of the hallway when an idea occurred to her. Ben was right—at this point she had no actual proof that Iris and Tristan had had an affair. It was nothing but gossip, and possibly nothing more than the prurient fantasy of Edmond Nugent. But she stubbornly believed that the affair was the key to everything, if it was true, and so she needed proof before she could go on to the next step. (Just like making pastry, she thought with a chuckle.)

Obviously confronting Tristan directly was unlikely to be

productive; he would almost certainly deny everything unless she could show him something he couldn't explain away. She needed something tangible, something he couldn't make an excuse for. *Hmm.*

His office. *That* was the place to look. She was willing to bet that Tristan's desk at the school had something in it that would give her the proof she and Ben needed—a note, a letter, a photograph, anything. Lovers are like magpies, collecting little bits of this and that, treasures and tokens to mark their love. Since Séverin was married, his office seemed the likely place to find them.

But she needed backup, or a lookout, or just a comrade-in-law-breaking. Who else but Frances? Molly tried her cell again but still got no answer, so she made sure Bobo's water bowl was full and then hopped on the scooter and sped to Nico's on rue Pasteur.

Castillac was still beautiful in the heat, though the light glared off the cobblestones and the golden limestone was so bright it hurt her eyes. The streets were empty and quiet. She felt sorry for the shopkeepers with all their customers staying home out of the heat, no one venturing out except for necessities.

Molly banged on Nico's door. His place was in a renovated stable, an ancient building with *colombages* on the second floor. No answer.

What the heck? Frances was usually busy writing jingles or lolling around with a book at this time of day. Where could she be?

She drove back to Chez Papa, thinking she and Nico would have to be there. She parked right by the door and gratefully went in out of the sun. "Nico! I've been trying to find Frances for hours. Where is she?"

Nico shook his head. "Oh, Molls." And then he put his face in his hands and moaned.

Molly's knees felt weak. "What? Has something happened?"

"Yes, wait, no," he said, collecting himself. "She's okay now. Yes, something did happen. I got Frances some flowers—she's so adorable, she really likes getting flowers, you know? And she put them in a vase just like you showed her and then she sort of croaked out my name and fell in a heap on the floor. Thank God I didn't think she was joking! I called the ambulance right away and thank God again they came quick—at first I thought maybe it was a reaction to the flowers somehow, but no, it was a bee. A bee came inside on the bouquet, stung her, and she had an allergic reaction."

"Anaphylactic shock?" Molly spoke in English, having no idea how to translate that.

"That is it," said Nico. "I tell you, Molly—it was the most terrifying thing I've ever seen. Frances is always pale but after the sting, her skin was like marble. She couldn't breathe, she was sweating...absolutely terrifying."

"But she's all right? Where is she now?"

"I insisted she come to work with me. She's in the back room."

Molly ran in to see Frances lying down in a banquette, reading on her tablet.

"Franny? What the hell?"

"I nearly died!" Frances said brightly as she sat up. "Nico was amazing. He didn't waste a second! And a good thing, too—the ambulance guy said that if he hadn't called that quickly, I'd be pushing up daisies."

Molly was speechless. She hugged her friend and didn't want to let go. "Do not die on me," she murmured. "I...I'm nowhere near ready for that."

"Me neither," said Frances, kissing her on the forehead. "I don't remember much of what happened. I arranged the roses, I remember the sting—and the next thing I know I'm waking up on the floor with faces peering down at me. Scared the crap out of Nico," she added, grinning.

"You look like you rather enjoyed the whole thing."

"Well, sometimes things in Castillac can get a little same-old same-old, am I right? It's not terrible to have a little drama that ends well. Especially if you get to see your man in action. Like a knight on a white charger, that was my Nico!"

Molly just shook her head. "So, are you all okay now? Not supposed to be on bed rest or anything?"

"Do I see a glint in your eye?"

"Maybe. I've got a little...escapade in mind. I thought of you first, naturally."

"Oh, this does sound good. We'll have to sneak out the back way—Nico's being so sweet but a little overprotective. So what? What evil plan have you been cooking up?"

"Not evil. But we'll have to kill time until dark."

"It's sounding better and better. Go get a kir and come back and tell me *everything*."

"I DON'T UNDERSTAND," Tristan Séverin was saying to Caroline, whose back was turned to him. "We've always gotten on so well, the two of us. Have I done something to upset you?"

Caroline turned to face him, glaring. "Yes. You have. But for a number of very good reasons, I do not want to discuss it. Can we just get back to work, please?" She sat down in her chair, her back straight. "I'll get over it," she said, waving a hand in the air.

Tristan kept looking at her quizzically. He needed a haircut and his shirt was wrinkled. "All right, Caroline," he said softly. "But if you change your mind, I'm happy to talk about whatever it is. I want the air to be clear between us."

Caroline answered with a flurry of typing, her fingers flying over the keyboard so quickly that Tristan thought for a moment she was faking it, just typing gibberish. But it was not gibberish, it was the report that Tristan should have finished last week but forgotten about, and Caroline, as she often did, was taking care of it for him.

"I'm a little at loose ends, with the children gone," he mused, looking out at the empty playground.

Caroline did not answer but kept clacking away at a furious pace.

Tristan got up and spent some minutes looking at the books on the bookshelf. "It's definitely something I did? I know things have been a little complicated around here lately, but we've been friends for so long, Caroline."

"Tristan!" shouted Caroline, raising her voice at work for the first time in her life. "Just leave it alone, will you?"

"Hector was supposed to fix that sink in the cantine. I'm going to go check on it," he said. He left the door open and crossed the scorching hot playground to the cantine. No lights were on and he kept it that way. He stood just inside the door, remembering Iris, how she would come out of the kitchen and greet the children as they came in, telling them about the day's menu, teasing them about this or that.

He remembered how she had smiled at him so shyly sometimes, her lashes lowered, like a character from a Jane Austen novel. He closed his eyes, willing her to be alive, magically there in the cantine with him.

Every minute she looked so beautiful, so full of life. Her hair curly from the humidity of the kitchen, her cheeks rosy, always with that white apron on, tied around her slender waist. His Iris. He didn't think he would ever get over losing her. It was beyond tragic. And now, to have to go home to his wife, with no Iris to look forward to, not ever...it was almost too much to bear.

He heard a clanking sound from the kitchen and went in to see if Hector had for once in his life done what he was supposed to do.

❧ 22 ❧

They had to wait until well after ten, it stayed so light in July. Molly wore a pair of navy blue shorts and a black T-shirt, and Frances a swirling black skirt with a dark gray camisole.

"I'm not sure you're dressed appropriately," said Molly.

"I'm thinking ahead to when we get arrested for breaking and entering. It's good to make a glamorous entrance, when you get hauled off to the station. And honestly, where'd you get the idea that navy blue and black were a smoking combination?"

Molly rolled her eyes. "Okay, let's go. I think we should walk. We'll be less noticeable than if we take the scooter."

They set off down rue des Chênes towards the school, Molly explaining to Frances what she hoped to find and the role she wanted Frances to play.

"Does Ben know about this plan?" asked Frances.

"Not exactly."

"You know we really could get arrested for this."

"You saying you can't handle it?"

"Ha! Of course not. I'm only wondering if *you* can handle it."

"We're not going to get caught," Molly said with confidence.

"What if the school is locked up tight? Are you planning to break windows? Is there an alarm system?"

"You have so little faith in me."

"What are you hinting about?"

"You'll see. I...did a bit of prep work earlier today."

"You've got crowbars and lock picks stashed under a bush?"

"I wish I knew how to pick locks. Seems like a handy skill to have."

"You don't have the patience for it."

"I don't disagree. Isn't the village amazing at this hour? So peaceful. I'm still startled by how different it is, here in France."

"I'm still startled that I came for month-long visit and haven't left yet."

Molly began humming "Isn't it Romantic." Frances elbowed her in the ribs.

The two women walked for a while in silence, winding their way through Castillac, listening to the clink of dishes as villagers finished up their dinner, the murmur of television, punctuated by the occasional cry of a baby. Swallows swooped through the darkening sky and they heard the scrape of plates and murmuring conversations. It was so beautiful in its ordinariness, and Molly could hardly believe that underneath the calm, only last week, passions in the village had risen up and up and all the way to murder.

"Here we go," said Molly, as they turned a corner and the school came into view. "You still in?"

"Of course I'm still in." Frances looked the building over. "Nice-looking place. You sure no one's going to show up for some after-hours catching up on paperwork or anything?"

"Um, 95% sure. In the summer there's only Tristan, Caroline, and maybe the plumber, and obviously none of them are here now. I think we're good."

Modern and one-story, the school stretched almost the length of the block. The playground was an interior courtyard, nothing fancy, with the cantine on the facing side. The classrooms and office building had large windows on the street and playground sides, keeping the rooms bright during the day and not affording much privacy from either direction.

Molly led Frances to a gate at the end of the block that opened onto the playground. The cantine was to the right and she glanced at it, and then walked to the school building and opened the door.

"How did you know this would be unlocked?" said Frances suspiciously.

"Duct tape," said Molly, grinning and pointing at the latchbolt, which was held back with a neatly applied section of silver tape.

"How did you—"

"You know how serious lunch is in France, right? I just waited until Caroline and Tristan had left to eat—it was easy to spy on them through the window, and school's out so there aren't any teachers or students around—and strolled in and taped the door. They don't lock up during the day, just at the end of the day when they go home. Actually, I don't even know that for sure—I get the feeling people in Castillac mostly don't bother locking their doors. Maybe the school is the same? I wanted to be on the safe side."

"I had no idea you had actual burglar skills. I bow down to you," said Frances.

They heard a noise and froze.

They were just inside the door, standing in the corridor, their silhouettes easily visible from either the playground or the street. Instinctively they ducked down, though the windows went so low their backs were still visible.

A scraping sound, metal on concrete, footsteps.

Frances peeked out of the street-side window. "It's just someone dragging a garbage can down the sidewalk," she whispered. "Which is pretty sketchy behavior, actually. Maybe we should tail him."

Molly took a big breath and stood up straight. "Okay, let's get this over with. I'm on the brink of having a heart attack."

They crept into the office. Not much light came in from the street so Molly pulled out her phone and tapped on the flashlight app so she could see what she was doing.

"Molls, that jiggling light is going to look mighty suspicious from the street...."

Molly gasped and shut it off. She hadn't really thought about how exposed a position the office was in. "I was so focused on getting inside, I didn't really think about how anyone walking by can see us."

"Just do this," said Frances, moving to Tristan's desk. She wiggled the mouse and the monitor came on, casting a soft glow over them.

"Brilliant!" whispered Molly. "Okay—you keep watch while I rifle through his drawers."

Frances giggled.

"Oh shut up," said Molly, laughing too. She opened the long narrow drawer first. It was so filled with stuff that it didn't slide out easily. Paper clips, pens, broken pencils, erasers, a bottle of liquid ink, ink cartridges, rubber bands, a couple of twigs, a crumpled pack of cigarettes, a lipstick.

A lipstick?

"Well," said Molly, holding it up. "Either Tristan likes a bit of cross-dressing, or this belonged to Iris," she said. "Highly doubt it's his wife's."

"Hundred per cent agree. Could it be DNA-tested?"

"No idea. But having her lipstick—is that even very damning? He could cook up an innocent story to explain it so easily. You know—'I ran into her at the market, noticed it on the ground after she'd moved on...'"

A row of three drawers was on the right, and Molly opened the first. It was crammed with papers and ink cartridges for a printer. She opened the second. "Definite hoarder tendencies,"

Molly reported, lifting out a dirty yogurt container. "Is the coast still clear?"

"I'll tell you if it's not," said Frances, chewing on a fingernail.

The third drawer was filled with books. Molly took out the top one, a slim book of poetry by Louis Aragon. A slip of paper poked out, and Molly opened the book to see what it was.

"Molly!" whispered Frances. "People coming down the street!" She scrambled over to Caroline's desk and hunched down behind it.

Molly dropped to the floor, hoping that the glow of Tristan's computer didn't give her away.

They heard talking. Someone began to sing. It felt as though it took forever for them to go past. Molly held her breath, imagining sirens and then Maron slapping handcuffs on her.

Ben shaking his head, not amused. Maybe even furious.

But slowly the sound of footsteps got fainter. Whoever it was stopped singing.

"Just hurry up, will you?" said Frances. "Aren't you finding anything?"

"Not so far," whispered Molly. "His desk is a mess!"

She stood up, crouching into the light of the computer, and looked at the slip of paper. "Well, now," she said.

"What? What is it?"

"A love poem. With Iris's name in it."

"Excellent, Inspector! Do you need more time? All's clear for the moment...."

"Just want to check to make sure it's his handwriting. An impossible chicken-scratch, let me tell you." Molly flipped through more papers until she found some hand-written notes in the margin. Yep, looks like his handwriting all right. Okay, we can go as soon as I go through these last drawers." Pause. "Shut up, Franny."

"I'm getting jumpy. Come on, let's get out of here."

Molly considered for a moment and decided that the poem

was enough. It did mention Iris's name, after all, and it was amorous enough that no one could mistake it as being simply about friendship. Carefully she closed the drawers all the way, though some papers still stuck out of the top of the bottom one. She slid the poem into the pocket of her shorts and joined Frances at the door.

Once they got to the playground, they ran. The fear of being seen, even arrested, caught up with them and all they wanted was to get as far away from the scene of the crime as possible. About five blocks later, they stopped, panting, and Molly took out the poem so they could read it under a streetlight.

"Eh, my French still isn't quite there. To put it mildly," said Frances, giving up quickly.

"Huh," said Molly, still studying it. The poem consisted of three stanzas of rather short lines. It did not rhyme. The handwriting was childish and messy, but legible.

And the poem was, if Molly's French was at all reliable, very erotic. Graphic in its description of what the writer wanted to do with Iris physically. Love was mentioned. The writer seemed on the point of being completely overwhelmed by the depth of his feelings for her.

On the one hand, the poem was fairly hilarious in its raw frankness. And on the other, well, Molly could see the appeal in being desired so fiercely. Who wouldn't?

❧ 23 ❧

"It's sort of a lust poem, if there's such a thing. But still pretty romantic in a way, don't you think?" said Molly to Ben as they had breakfast at the Café de la Place. Ben's hair was still damp from the shower after his morning run, but the exercise had apparently not done much to relax him.

"I don't care how you characterize it, that doesn't change the fact that you stole something from that office," said Ben. Molly waited for him to smile but he did not. "I thought you said you had made something of a career out of watching American crime shows. Didn't you learn that evidence gained through illegal means is ruined? Inadmissible?"

Molly was chastened but did not want to admit it. "Listen. If I hadn't gotten my mitts on this poem, we still wouldn't know that Iris's lover was 99% for sure Tristan Séverin. All right, point taken, we can't hand it over to Maron and get it booked into evidence. But we can still use it as leverage. Pretty powerful leverage, if you ask me. I bet you anything Séverin folds like a cheap accordion when you show him this poem."

"Maybe." Ben glowered at his coffee, his arms folded across his chest. "Then there's the issue of breaking and entering."

"We didn't break anything! Although in retrospect we probably should have worn gloves."

Ben did not smile. "I want you to understand, Molly. We cannot be partners if you're going to continue breaking the law."

"Do you mean...partners in detective work? Or any kind of partners?"

"I meant the investigation. But...."

She saw, suddenly and too late, that her illegal snooping had crossed a line, and that he felt her action to be not only illegal, but disrespectful to him. Instead of continuing to defend herself, Molly let loose a flood of heartfelt apologies, promising that the next time she had a big idea for collecting evidence, she would run it by him first.

"I don't savor the prospect of visiting you in prison," he said, and finally with relief Molly saw a faint twinkle in his eye.

"Do you think Maron would really have arrested us, if Franny and I'd been caught? I'm not justifying, just curious."

"Yes, I do. And I think he'd have enjoyed it immensely." Ben leaned back in his chair, lost in thought. "And the new gendarme, Monsour? He's just itching to put someone in jail. It's a particular type that gets attracted to law enforcement—they savor the authoritarian part of it. Can spot it in Monsour a mile away."

"Ew."

Ben shrugged, and Molly couldn't help smiling at how supremely Gallic he seemed in the moment.

"So, here's a question..." continued Molly. "Why do you think Caroline lied to me?"

"She was adamant about Séverin not having any affairs?"

"Absolutely. Said she would definitely know, too."

Ben shrugged. "Who knows. Maybe nothing more than loyalty to her boss."

Molly sat in silence, eating her croissant. Then she erupted in laughter, startling the people at the next table. "I'm just...the poem! It's so *raunchy!*"

Ben smiled. "It's certainly not what I'd have expected Séverin to write. I've always thought of him as...an innocent, really. We need someone to look at his computer. I'll go talk to Maron after breakfast, make sure he's taking the school computer in and seeing what else might be on there. His emails might be a mother lode."

Molly nodded vigorously. "Oh, yeah, I'd love a look at Séverin's emails. And Iris's. Pierre's too, for that matter. Though I suppose it would be too much to hope for, finding something like, 'You humiliated me so I'm going to push you downstairs'."

"Probably," said Ben, not twinkling this time.

"YOU KNOW, for a couple, you and Dufort sure don't seem to spend much time together," said Lapin, standing next to Molly and Lawrence at the bar at Chez Papa Friday night. "I think our own Miss Marple might be back on the market soon, don't you, Larry?"

Lawrence raised an eyebrow but otherwise paid attention to his Negroni.

"I'm not biting on that piece of bait," said Molly cheerfully, although in spite of herself she felt a slight pang at the suggestion that something wasn't quite right between her and Ben. "It's just that he likes to stay in and read at the end of the day, and I like going out and seeing people. Even if you lot is all I can muster."

"Ouch," said Lawrence, grinning.

"Thought you weren't taking the bait, Sutton," said Lapin, grinning even harder.

"And I'm *not* Miss Marple, either. She had at least a few decades on me. Now, how about instead of talking about me, we talk about Iris. Lapin, you're usually right in the middle of any murders in Castillac. What's your angle this time?"

NELL GODDIN

"Very funny, Molly." Lapin took a long, dramatic sip of his beer.

"Did either of you know she was having an affair with Séverin?" asked Molly.

Lawrence didn't say anything but Molly could see *yes* in his eyes. Lapin looked disgusted. "I don't know why she didn't choose me," he said, rubbing one hand over his large belly. "I always thought we had a spark."

Molly and Lawrence smiled at each other.

"Do you think Pierre knew? Did it drive him to murder in a jealous rage?" she asked.

"Frankly, I've never seen Pierre in a rage about anything. Not even close. He is the most even-tempered of men, wouldn't you say?" said Lawrence.

Molly considered this. It was true that she'd never seen him lose his temper, but she hadn't spent much time with him either. She wanted to hear the impressions of those in the village who had grown up with him, who had seen him regularly for years and years.

In the back of her mind, she knew she was being stubborn, but she still felt sure he was guilty. The discovery of the affair with Séverin and the love poem only cemented her opinion. It was irritating that no one else seemed to share her certainty.

"So are you saying you *don't* think it was Pierre?" she asked.

Lawrence and Lapin drank their drinks and didn't answer at first.

"I'm going to give you my usual answer when you ask questions like these," said Lawrence finally. "I don't know. I don't know much of anything about anything, when you get down to it. I can't explain why Iris married Pierre in the first place. I can't explain why, of all the men she could have had, she chose Tristan Séverin. I can't explain why during her funeral, Pierre looked more bored than anything else."

"You saw that? I thought the same thing," said Lapin. "I swear, he never deserved her. Such a goddess...."

"That's the word everyone keeps using," said Molly. "Is it just a figure of speech, or did she actually not seem human?"

"I can't say. I never had the courage to say a word to her."

"If that's how a lot of people thought of her, she might have been very lonely," suggested Lawrence.

"Another round?" asked Nico, looking not very warmly at Molly. He was not pleased about the escapade at the school, worrying that Frances might have gotten caught and deported. Coming right on the heels of the bee incident, his nerves were a little frayed.

"So tomorrow is Changeover Day, right?" asked Lawrence. "Anyone new coming tomorrow?"

"Yes. The Hales are leaving and a Miss Eugenia Perry from Louisiana is coming, an older woman traveling by herself. Thanks for bringing it up, I need to text Constance to remind her to come. And...ugh, now that you've got me thinking about it, some of the tile is loose in the cottage bathroom. I really should go home right now and grout it, give it a night to cure. The Hales are so accommodating, I don't think they'll mind."

"Alas! I didn't mean to push you out the door."

"Oh, I know that," she said, kissing him on the forehead. "Sometimes my running of the gîte business gets a little lost in all the detective work, and if I don't watch my step, I'm going to have some unhappy guests."

"And no more gîte business," offered Lapin.

"Right. Okay, now you're making my blood run cold. Good night to you both! And, um, if you hear anything you think I might be interested in, pass it my way, will you?"

"Of course! Go attend to your grout," said Lawrence, waving to Nico and twirling his finger to signal another drink.

Molly was two steps from the door when Tristan Séverin came in.

"Oh!" said Molly, her face instantly red.

Having read the poem he wrote for Iris felt suddenly like such a violation, even though she wouldn't have taken back the burglary for anything.

Find some poise!

"Bonsoir, Tristan," she said. "I'm off to grout a bathroom. Have a good night, everyone!"

She hoped that hadn't sounded too false.

As she rode home on the scooter, Molly wasn't thinking about the grout, or her new guests, but instead wondering about Madame Séverin, and whether it was worth paying her a visit.

❧ 24 ❧

First thing Saturday morning, Molly jumped out of bed and started to go check on the grout in the cottage before she realized the Hales were probably still asleep, enjoying their final day at La Baraque. Guests fell into two camps: either they slept really late on the last day, trying to squeeze every bit of relaxation out of their vacation, or they got up early, anxious about getting everything done and being ready for the next leg of their trip.

As long as she was already up, Molly made coffee and drank a cup on the terrace. It was not so hot at that time of day, and Bobo was her usual rambunctious self. Molly picked up her phone and began to make a list of all the repairs and projects she wanted to do at La Baraque:

caulk the grouted tile in the cottage
figure out why the floor in the hallway has that soft spot
plant some fruit trees
rebuild barn

Well, shoot. If Pierre's in prison, that barn'll never get rebuilt, she thought, instantly appalled at her selfishness.

She heard the sound of tire on gravel, Bobo barked her head off, and Constance came around the side of the house.

"Bonjour, Molly!" she sang out, her hair scraped back in its usual work-ready ponytail.

"Bonjour Constance. You're early. Want some coffee? I haven't seen the Hales or Finsterman yet."

"I think Finsterman has moved in for good. He's never leaving."

"He does seem happy here. But I've got a couple staying in the pigeonnier in two weeks so he can't stay beyond that. If we see him, I thought we'd ask if we could duck in and give it a quick cleaning."

"Whatever you say, Boss," said Constance cheerfully.

"Things going well with Thomas?"

"I thought you'd never ask! We're talking about moving in together," she said, beaming.

"That's good? If you're happy, I'm happy," said Molly.

"Wait, what? You think it's a terrible idea?"

"I didn't say that!"

"'If you're happy, I'm happy'...everybody knows that really means 'you're making a terrible mistake but as long as you haven't figured that out yet, I'm not gonna say anything'."

Molly started chuckling and then fell into a full-on belly laugh. "You're brilliant, Constance," she said. "You nailed it. But honestly—truly—I didn't mean anything other than what I said. You *are* happy?"

Constance nodded vigorously.

"Then so am I. Really." She stood up and stretched. "Let's go see if anyone is stirring. I'd like to get the cleaning over with as soon as we can, and then run to the market. Doing things a bit backwards this time."

She didn't say that she was reluctant to go to Pâtisserie Bujold, now that Nugent would be expecting her to arrange the time for her next pastry lesson. She had only gone through with the first one to see if he knew whom Iris was having the affair with, and now that she knew, the last thing she wanted to do was spend another long evening with him and his double entendres. Although the delectable final result, hot from the oven, made almost any indignity worth it.

As she and Constance got out the vacuum, pails, and mop, she realized she felt a little rotten to have taken advantage of Nugent that way. She'd been a manipulative user, not to put too fine a point on it. All this investigating—it was certainly exciting and satisfying, but it also meant that sometimes she acted like a jerk.

But worth it, right? Molly thought. If I were Iris, wouldn't I be more than happy for people to behave badly if it meant capturing my killer? Moral purity is all fine and well but it's not very useful for getting anyone to talk.

The two women strolled over to the cottage. The orange cat was curled up on the front step, against the door, looking almost sweet as she slept. No sound from inside.

"I don't want to bother them—I already interrupted them last night. They've had enough inconvenience. Well, let's try the pigeonnier. I think Finsterman has usually left with his easel and paintbox by now."

"Just think, Molly. He could be a famous artist someday, talking about the inspiration he got at La Baraque!"

"Ha! I'm not sure Finsterman has such high ambitions. Though maybe I should suggest he look in at L'Institut Degas and see if it interests him. I'd be more than happy to have a long-term renter while he got through his studies."

Molly knocked on the door. No answer. She stepped back and gazed at the outside of the pigeonnier, noting, as she did every time, what an amazing job Pierre had done. It looked practically like Le Courbusier. The wall of the circular structure had a slight undulation that was pleasing, almost as though there was muscle under the skin of the wall—it made you want to skim your hand over it, to pet it. The building seemed practically alive. And at night, when the tiny windows were lit up from inside, it was absolutely magical. Whatever else he might be, Pierre was an artist, and an inspired one.

"Mr. Finsterman?" Molly called. "Like I said, I'm pretty sure he's out." She pushed the latch and stuck her head inside, calling again and getting no answer. "Okay Constance, come on in. I'll do the bathroom and kitchen, you do a quick dust and vacuum. We'll be out in a jiffy."

Constance nodded and went in with a handful of dustcloths while Molly went to the bathroom. "*Merde!*" she shouted. "Another leaky faucet! I swear these things are made to break after six months." She thought for a second. "Listen, I'm going to have to go get some washers, so I might as well do the marketing while I'm there. You want anything? You don't mind doing my part in here as well as yours?"

"Anything you say, Boss," said Constance, grinning.

Love, thought Molly, on her way to the scooter. When it's going well, it even makes cleaning bathrooms seem like fun.

FOR MOST OF THE CASTILLAÇOIS, Saturday was for household chores, for marketing, for visiting with friends, and cooking. Some would take long walks in the countryside, some would paint or write or read. But almost no one chose to work if their job did not require it.

Pierre was used to being the odd one out. In school he had done better than most of his mates, and though he got along with them well enough, he had not made any close friends. His history teacher had urged him to take the academic path, saying he had enough ability to teach at a university if he chose to— but Pierre knew he would be a terrible teacher, and besides, he had known what his life's work would be since he was very young.

Stones and rocks, walls and stairs. That was what he had loved for as long as he could remember. He was never happier than when absorbed in a project, the more complex the better, and to him it was great good luck that people would actually pay him to do work he enjoyed so deeply.

His tools were already at the Lafont's and so he needed little time to get ready—he had a quick cup of coffee, was in his truck by eight, and at the site by eight-fifteen. He had learned over the years that no matter how feverish a client was to have something finished, they got angry if he applied mallet to chisel before around ten on a Saturday morning. People were confusing, but eventually Pierre had simply accepted the contradiction and learned to work around it.

And in fact, like many artists, he had come to appreciate the restriction. Having to spend a few hours thinking through his plans, looking carefully at the stone he was going to use that day, but not allowing himself to do anything more—it made the desire to create build up inside him with a kind of pleasurable pressure. And on that particular Saturday, barely over a week since his wife died, the enjoyable anticipation was no different.

The Lafont house was not especially grand, which suited its owners. It was built in the sixteenth and seventeenth centuries, had tiny windows and so was quite dark inside, and had retained many of the details of those eras including a dry stone sink. Pierre understood the affection the couple had for their house. The stonework was obviously of a high order, having lasted for centuries with only minor repairs, and of course the golden Dordogne limestone was a favorite of his—to his mind, much more valuable and beautiful than having the light-filled rooms which were more the current style.

Dressed in a T-shirt and canvas shorts, he squatted down next to a pile of rocks and observed them. He let his eyes wander over them, noticing their topography, not allowing himself to touch them at first. Then he went inside the structure—it was an addition to the Lafont's house, so he could go in without bothering them—and inspected the stairs, which had been so tricky to get in place, since the stone was so heavy and the space for the stairs cramped.

When he was younger, Pierre had traveled around the département and beyond, visiting cathedrals and chateaux, anywhere that had stonework for him to study. He had taken Iris on many of these trips, although she generally gave the buildings only a cursory glance before going to whatever garden was nearby. It had been a disappointment to him that she did not understand his fascination with rocks.

At last it was ten o'clock, and with his fingers almost tingling at the prospect, he selected a chisel and picked up his mallet and went to work, nicking off a protrusion here, smoothing a rough patch there. He did not think about Iris, but only of the texture and shape of the stones he was working with, never losing sight of the way in which they would fit into his design.

He kept smacking mallet to chisel for several hours, until Madame Lafont thought she was on the brink of losing her mind, and Monsieur Lafont poured her a splash of Cognac to calm her down even though it was still before lunch.

MOLLY LEFT Constance in the pigeonnier, hopped on the scooter, and...nothing. The engine coughed, sputtered, and died. "Come on, now," she said to it, stroking the streaky paint on the gas tank. "Can't you just make it into the village? I promise I'll take you to the doctor first thing."

But the scooter showed no sign of life. Reminding herself that she had done just fine without any transportation for many months, she turned down rue des Chênes on foot, making a list in her mind of everything she needed to do.

A storm was coming. The sky over half the village was dark and threatening, and a hot breeze had picked up. Molly walked faster, plotting the route of her chores, and telling herself not to stop and chat too long with everyone.

But Rémy had the best tomatoes by far, and he was always so interesting to talk to—she didn't know anyone else who relished a conversation about manure as much as she and Rémy did. Of course she had to hear all about what Manette was up to, how her perennially sick mother-in-law was doing, and her pack of children as well. By the time she was ready to go to Pâtisserie Bujold and talk to Nugent, she was loaded down with food and it was over two hours later, but at least the rain hadn't come yet.

She had found out the Séverin's address earlier, and thought she'd pass by their house—it was on the way to the pastry shop, after all—just to see if by any chance Madame Séverin was home and willing to answer a few questions.

Well, since the woman was agoraphobic, it was a pretty good bet she was home. But was she home alone, and would she talk? Molly wasn't sure she was willing to be a total jerk and grill someone she'd never met—and a depressive—about her husband's love life. She didn't really know what she was after, just figured that the more people she talked to that had some connection to Iris, even indirectly, the better she would understand how the beautiful woman had ended up getting shoved down the stairs.

Molly had so many bags that she had to stop every once in a while to readjust and flex her hands. She turned onto rue Saterne and saw Madame Tessier sitting in her usual chair beside her front door, watching everything that happened on her street.

"Bonjour, Madame Tessier," said Molly. "How have you been?"

"Bonjour Molly," the old lady said, furrowing her brows. "You know, it just occurred to me that your arrival in the village was when all these murders started happening. I think you might be very bad luck!"

Molly was taken aback until she saw that Madame Tessier was joking.

"So tell me how your investigation is going," the old woman asked. "And don't try telling me you're not working on it. I already know you've been talking to people around the village, and that you think Iris's husband is the killer."

Molly grinned. "You do have good information," she said. "Very impressive. Well, I'm all ears if you have any other ideas besides Pierre. You know I have the highest respect for your opinion." Molly had guessed the first time she met Madame Tessier that she was susceptible to flattery, and she was not wrong.

"I wonder if perhaps you are jumping to that conclusion simply because there are so many bad husbands in the world," Madame Tessier said. "My Albert, he is nothing at all like that. Gentle as a lamb, and very loving too," she said, with a waggle of her neatly-plucked eyebrows.

Molly laughed. "You are lucky. Well, I've no doubt that Maron and the new gendarme, Monsour I believe he's called, are taking statements and interviewing witnesses, and maybe that will sort out the possibilities further. I hear Pierre's alibi is a little shaky."

"Ben tells you everything? Yes, of course I know Pierre hired him," she said, throwing her head back and cackling. "Molly! I know *everything* that goes on in this village!"

"So then tell me—who killed Iris?"

Madame Tessier looked irritated. "I'm not going to say. It's early yet. I'll say this, however: if it turns out to have been Pierre, I will be very surprised indeed."

Molly thanked her for the chat and said goodbye, turning left on rue des Anges in search of the Séverin's house.

And just then the skies opened, all at once, and Molly turned around and ran for the shelter of Pâtisserie Bujold. Well, there are worse places to wait out a rainstorm, she thought, already anticipating sipping a hot espresso and lingering over the display case, trying to decide what to have with it.

Maybe Edmond will tell me who gave him the information on Séverin, she thought. And maybe...maybe in this case, it would turn out that who told him will be more important that what he was told.

❧ 25 ❧

On Monday morning Ben and Molly headed over to the school, wanting to confront the principal directly about his affair with Iris and see what he had to say for himself. "That's Séverin's car, right?" asked Molly, pointing at a blue Citroën in the school parking area.

"I think so." Ben swerved over and peered inside. "Untidy," he said.

"I want to come look but I don't want him to see us. He lives in the village, right? Why would he drive, in weather this nice?"

Dufort shrugged. "Ask him."

They passed the school office window and could see Caroline and Séverin inside at their desks. Dufort had a momentary pang of wishing he were still chief gendarme, in possession of the deference and authority that came with the position.

"Excuse me," he said to them, knocking on the opened door to the office. "I'm sorry to interrupt. Do you have a moment to talk to us?"

"I'm afraid there is a deadline looming just ahead, and Monsieur Séverin is in danger of missing it. Perhaps another time—"

"Oh, Caroline, I'm sure we'll make it, not to worry. Come on in, Madame Sutton, Ben. Have a seat! We hardly have anything to do during vacation, as you might imagine. Really we just twiddle our thumbs until the children come back and this place comes alive again," he said, gesturing to the playground. "All right then, what's on your minds?" He leaned back comfortably in his chair and put his hands behind his head.

"As you know, we're investigating Iris Gault's death. And there are some discrepancies we'd like to clear up, just a few little things to help us get a clearer picture of what happened," said Ben.

"I'm going to step out for a moment, Monsieur Séverin," said Caroline. "We've run out of—"

"Mademoiselle Dubois," interrupted Dufort, "I would ask that you stay. I am no longer an officer, as you know, so I cannot force you. But I ask for that small favor, on Iris's behalf."

Caroline sank slowly back to her seat.

Everyone waited for Dufort to continue, but he felt a little off balance in his new capacity as a private investigator. He recognized that his role was different but he hadn't quite found his voice and wasn't sure how to proceed.

Molly blurted out, "Well, you'll understand that if we're trying to figure out who killed Iris, we need to know what was going on with her before she died. How she spent her time, the state of her marriage, that sort of thing." She paused, glanced at Dufort, and jumped the rest of the way. "We're asking you to confirm that you were in a romantic relationship with Iris, Monsieur Séverin."

Séverin sighed. "With Iris? Who in the world told you that?"

"You know how it is in the village," said Dufort. "People keep an eye out. They talk."

A silence, while Molly and Ben waited to see if either of them would be forthcoming. They were not.

"And...there's the matter of this poem," said Molly, holding the slip of paper out so they could see what it was.

ꙮ

CAROLINE LET out a strangled sob and then she was up out of her chair, pacing in front of the window. Ben and Molly watched her, their eyes wide.

"Where did you get that?" she said, with an angry glance at Séverin. "Is there no privacy anymore? People are allowed to just take whatever they want and pass it around? There are no *rules?*"

Séverin bowed his head and then looked at Caroline tenderly.

"It's *my* poem," said Caroline. "I wrote it, though I never intended for Iris—or anyone—to read it. Obviously it's...it's very private." There were tears glittering in the corners of her eyes but she was defiant. "But listen. I'm not ashamed to say...if you've read it, you already know—I *loved* her. Along with half the village. Yes, I loved Iris Gault with all my heart. Which as far as I know is no one else's business and certainly no crime."

Ben and Molly were stunned.

"*You* wrote it?" Molly finally said, wonderingly.

"You were friends with Iris?" Dufort asked gently.

"Yes, we were friends, of *course* we were friends. She worked here in the cantine, as you very well know. I saw her every single school day for three years. I ate lunch with her, took breaks with her, had coffee every afternoon with her. She was beautiful, that was the most obvious thing about her, no one could miss that. But she was far more than just beautiful. She was interested in so many things. So warm. Complicated. She was...." Caroline put her face in her hands.

"But you were the one sleeping with her," said Molly to Séverin with her Yankee directness.

He shook his head, then raised his palms and shrugged. "I sent her some flowers, that's all," he admitted. "She was crazy for flowers."

"But more than that—you were in a romantic and sexual relationship with her, isn't that right?" Molly followed up, feeling a bit like a reporter for a tabloid.

"Please," said Séverin, glancing at his distraught assistant. "Haven't we had enough for one morning? Iris was my *friend*. My good friend. And Caroline and I are both mourning her very deeply."

Dufort ran his tongue over his teeth, considering. "Molly, any more questions right now?"

Molly shook her head.

"If you have nothing more for me, I'd like to go to the bathroom, if I may," said Caroline.

"Go ahead," said Dufort. He noticed that her face was splotchy and her eyes puffy, and wondered if she had been crying before he and Molly arrived.

Molly and Ben thanked Séverin and made their way outside. They held hands, gripping tightly to communicate silently to each other their surprise at what they had heard. When they had gotten three long blocks away, Molly burst out, "Wow! *Caroline* wrote that poem? And you know, I felt so dumb once she said it. It *had* to have been written by a woman. It's perfectly obvious once that possibility is an option. I just *assumed*…and assuming is the very thing I keep telling myself to stop doing."

"Things are looking a little better for your guy," added Molly. "Even if Tristan and Iris were just friends, which I'm not necessarily convinced was the case—how about Caroline? Some very powerful emotions there. I don't like to admit it, but the suspect field has gotten a little more crowded."

Ben slipped his arm around and pulled her in for a kiss, right there on the street in the middle of the day.

❧ 26 ❧

He didn't want to do it. Maron stood in his office at the station, staring at his phone as though he expected it would suddenly begin talking, and tell him what he should do next.

Pull yourself together, man.

He tapped Dufort's number.

"Bonjour, Ben," he said, managing to sound confident. "I'm wondering if you have some time this morning for a quick consultation. It's the Gault case. Thought we were right on top of it—just about to make an arrest. But it turns out our prime suspect has an alibi, a tight one."

Ben had anticipated that Maron would call eventually, if the case didn't resolve quickly. The man had little patience, and Ben was not fooled by his swaggering tone—he knew perfectly well that being acting chief had thrown Maron for a major loop, and he had not regained his footing even months later.

"I'd be happy to talk things over. Shall I come right now?"

❧

MOLLY HAD STARTED the walk home alone, mulling over the interview with Caroline and Tristan. With some regret, she believed Caroline had written the poem, even though she hadn't seen it coming. But still, something didn't sit right about the whole thing. Had Nugent been wrong about Iris and Tristan? And if so, where had he gotten his bad information?

And what about Pierre? Did he realize the village gossip lines were humming with talk about his wife and the school principal, even if it wasn't true?

Molly wound her way through an alley. Idly she picked up a stick and tapped it on things as she walked along. Bang on a garbage can. Whap on a picket fence. Thump on the side of a garage.

The village was preternaturally quiet, as though gathering itself up in silence for some kind of explosion, or earthquake. She heard no conversation, no movement, not so much as a dog scratching.

Then footsteps, someone running behind her.

"Tristan?" she said, seeing him hurry towards her.

"Madame Sutton!" he said. He stopped when he reached her, panting lightly. "I may call you Molly?"

She nodded, curious.

"Well, I...I'm glad I caught up with you. I'm...would you mind if I walked a little way with you? I have some things to add to what we were talking about before."

"Of course."

"It's, well..." Tristan laughed nervously. "It's embarrassing, is what it is. I felt—well, a wide assortment of things, actually, but mainly I did not want to hurt Caroline anymore than she already has been, if you understand."

Molly stopped. "Yes?"

"Unrequited love can be so terribly painful, you know. I've been there—I suspect we all have."

Molly nodded, curious.

"So—I apologize for not being forthcoming, it was like something grabbed me by the throat and would not allow me to speak."

Molly waited. The only sound was a cicada buzzing in a nearby tree.

"The truth is...I *was* seeing Iris. Romantically, I mean. It's... well, let me tell you how it was. Iris and I spent so much time together over the years. Lunch every school day, consulting on the management of the cantine... naturally, a bond develops, you understand. My own marriage, well, I try to do right by my wife, I honestly do, but...oh, I can't excuse what I've done. I make no excuses. It was just that one day, suddenly—do you know the term *coup de foudre*, Molly? Literally, in English it is 'thunderbolt'. A term for what you call 'love at first sight'. It was not like that for Iris and me— what we had developed slowly, over years—but it was a lightning bolt all the same. Out of nowhere it seemed. Impossible to resist."

Molly smiled ruefully, remembering a *coup de foudre* of her own many years ago. "And you're saying you kept back this information out of concern for Caroline?"

"Partly. In the moment I wanted to spare her that extra bit of pain. But if I am completely honest, I was surprised by the question and just blurted out 'no' without thinking. Used to hiding it, you see, out of respect for our spouses. But I have no wish to do anything that might get in the way of your investigation, so after a moment's reflection, I chased you down in this alleyway to set the record straight." He smiled and shrugged. "I'm sorry."

"Thank you for your honesty. I assume I can pass this on to Ben?"

"Of course! You know we have a different attitude toward affairs here in France. It's not necessarily—not always—a thing to get in a moral outrage over, the way I believe it is in the States. Am I correct about that?"

"Depends."

"No doubt. Well, I don't claim to be…I just…Molly, she was so very beautiful, inside and out. I am just grateful to have had that time with her. I'm not sure I'll ever get over her loss."

They exchanged a few sentences about grief and then about the weather, and Tristan retraced his steps back to the school as Molly turned onto rue des Chênes. She stopped to text Ben to tell him of Séverin's confession, and then headed for home.

I knew it. Since when has Lawrence's information ever been wrong?

BEN DIDN'T THINK Maron would allow Molly to sit in on the meeting—it was humiliating enough to have to ask Ben for help, much less a civilian. He wasted no time getting to the station, where he found Maron alone. Skipping any preliminaries, Maron got straight to it. "Let me lay it out for you," said Maron, half-sitting on Monsour's desk. "The husband, Pierre—he's the obvious suspect, right? He found the body. His alibi does cover much of the time frame Nagrand gives us, but this is not a time-consuming murder, all he needs is a few seconds to shove her downstairs. An alibi is no good at all as long as there's a big enough sliver of time when the crime could have been committed."

Dufort nodded patiently.

"Sorry for thinking out loud, I know none of what I'm saying is news to you," said Maron. "I assume Pierre's told you about the insurance money? It's not an insubstantial sum, Dufort. We've been unable to find anyone who will tell us anything about the state of their marital relationship, but the money is incriminating. Easily a good enough motive for Pierre to have killed her."

"So it's Pierre you were about to charge?"

"No, no. My reasoning is that if you were going to murder your wife for an insurance payout, that's a premeditated sort of crime, right? Not a situation where the perpetrator gets carried away in the heat of the moment, a murder of passion. And so if you've got time to think about it, wouldn't it make a lot more sense to take steps to hide your guilt? For one thing, a push down the stairs could very well not be fatal. With better luck, she might have jumped up with nothing more than a bruise or two—and called us and had him taken in for battery.

"In addition, Pierre is alone in the house with the corpse when Monsour shows up. There's no evidence that anyone else had been there. He said he called the ambulance but the phone records don't back him up. All the circumstances point to Pierre being the one with motive, means, and opportunity. If you're devising a way to get an insurance payout, that would be the most ill-conceived plan ever devised." Maron narrowed his eyes at Dufort while waiting for his reaction, hoping very much that he would nod and agree.

"All right, said Dufort slowly. "Let me see if I understand you. In effect, you're saying that you don't think it was Pierre, because Pierre looks so guilty?"

To his horror Maron felt a blush creeping up his neck. "Not precisely, sir. Let me continue. Without ruling out Pierre for all the reasons stated, we've been looking at someone else, someone who might very well have had a more, shall we say, *ardent* relationship with the deceased, and for whom a momentary loss of control would be more understandable, psychologically speaking."

Dufort felt like rolling his eyes even though what Maron said had at least a whisper of merit. He was happy to hear any line of thought that helped to keep Pierre on the sidelines of the investigation.

Just then, his phone vibrated and he drew it out and glanced at the screen.

tristan ran after me. changed story. yes to affair after all

Dufort was surprised, but more by Tristan's admission than the fact of the affair.

NELL GODDIN

Maron continued, "We believe that Iris Gault was having an affair with Tristan Séverin. You know him, of course?"

Dufort nodded, saying nothing about the text. "Not well. But yes, we're acquaintances."

"We were postulating that Iris had broken it off with him, and in reaction, he got violent. You have something going on with the most desirable woman in the village, you're not going to want to let go, right? I know, I know—he works with children, for God's sake. But since when does having a respectable, peaceful sort of job mean that a man can't have passions, even passions that turn homicidal?"

"His assistant says there was no affair," said Dufort, toying with him a little.

"What? I don't see how that's proof of anything."

"Assistants always know that sort of thing. People, generally, are bad at keeping secrets. I would guess Séverin especially, given how much he likes to talk. He's just a centimeter short of being a windbag, is my experience with him. Amiable, I grant you. But a talker."

Maron looked down at the floor, pressing his lips together.

"And like you say—if he was sleeping with the famous Iris Gault, the woman every man wanted—don't you think he'd wish everyone knew about it? Such a badge of macho honor."

Maron stood up and flexed his shoulders. Dufort could see he had been working out, including lifting weights; Maron's uniform was straining across his biceps and he looked very lean and strong.

"How did you hear about the affair?" asked Dufort, feeling a bit remorseful for torturing poor Maron.

"Tessier."

"Ah. Well, I've never known her to steer me wrong. So it's Séverin in your crosshairs now?"

"Let me tell you the rest of it, I haven't even gotten to the reason I called. So, as I said, we were looking hard at Séverin, figuring he might have a strong motive as well as opportunity. But

170

we interviewed the assistant, Caroline Dubois, who says she was out for a walk that Friday night, 11 July, and saw Séverin in the office, working late. You know how those school windows are, it's like being in a fishbowl. And his car was parked out front. We asked around and found two other villagers who gave exactly the same evidence. It's been so hot lately that I guess people are out walking after dark more than usual.

"The time span covering those accounts gives the man an air-tight alibi. I can say without reservation, unfortunately, that Tristan Séverin did not commit this murder. Obviously that turns us back to Pierre. Tomorrow morning we're going to bring him in for a little chat."

Dufort felt an icy jolt of anxiety and felt in his pocket for his vial of tincture. "But you just ran through a list of reasons why you didn't believe it was Pierre," he said, cocking his head. "Okay then, Séverin is out. But it occurs to me that Iris's murderer wouldn't have to be someone in a romantic relationship with her. It could just as easily be someone who wanted her but could not have her."

"From what I hear, that could be half the village."

Dufort shrugged. "Obviously she was extremely attractive. And private, too, kept herself apart a little bit. Not in a snobbish way, but mysterious somehow. Anyway, I'm simply suggesting that you not limit your list of suspects to those proven to have a romantic connection with her. Wanting someone desperately and being rejected—that can be a powerful stimulus to very bad behavior."

Maron nodded as if to say he had this angle covered, then said, "What have you got, Dufort? You're thinking of someone in particular, I can see that much."

Dufort sighed a little theatrically. "How about Caroline Dubois?"

Maron's eyes got ridiculously wide. "You mean—"

"She had feelings for Iris that went beyond friendship.

Possibly verging on obsessive. Have a chat with her, Maron. And... of course you've taken Caroline and Tristan's computers, at work and home?" Dufort asked.

"Of course," answered Maron, a little too quickly. He waited until Dufort had gone and quickly made some phone calls.

✌ 27 ✌

Ms. Eugenia Perry, from Slidell, Louisiana, had immediately proven herself to be the sort of guest any gîte owner would be thrilled to have. She arrived at La Baraque in a taxi at the height of the afternoon storm, when Molly was indulging in a few madeleines and a second espresso at Pâtisserie Bujold. Eugenia had gone straight into the cottage and made herself at home, and greeted Molly with delight when she finally straggled in, soaked to the skin and overly caffeinated.

Eugenia's understanding and good humor notwithstanding, Molly wanted to make it up to her guest, so she invited her to breakfast later in the week. Happily that Tuesday dawned sunny and temperate, and all the creatures at La Baraque, human and animal, were in better spirits now that the heat wave had broken.

Molly was mournful about the scooter. Having no idea what the repairs would cost, she was hesitant to take it to the shop. And of course she missed zipping into the village to get fresh croissants in a matter of minutes. She did know how to make them herself now, thanks to Nugent, but croissants took a long time—the dough had to rest for hours between all the foldings and poundings. Eugenia was going to have to make do with an omelet.

Soon enough the two women were seated at the rusty table on the terrace, Bobo and the orange cat hanging out hopefully at their feet, with glasses of freshly squeezed orange juice and two glistening buttery omelets scattered with snips of tarragon and chives from the garden.

"I'm glad to see you're an eater," said Eugenia, taking an enormous bite.

Molly nearly choked on her food. "That's the understatement of the year," she said. "It's one of the best things about living here —life revolves around food. Everyone in Castillac is thinking about it, planning it, cooking it, or eating it pretty much every waking moment."

"I don't know if you've ever been down Louisiana way, but we know a little about cooking too. Ever had crab with remoulade sauce, or a shrimp étouffée?"

"No, but just the poetic sound of those words is making my mouth water. If I thought we could get the ingredients, I might be pushing you into the kitchen to take care of dinner!"

Eugenia laughed. "I can't believe I'm really here," she said, looking around. "It's my first time out of the country. I'll tell you, I've had a lucky life. I didn't get much in the way of schooling, grew up working on my family's farm deep in the bayou. But I was a pretty thing, when I was young—no, I really was!" she laughed, patting her round belly. "I married a rich man and he died and left me every single penny. So I've spent the last fifteen years reading books and eating the most delicious food I can, just enjoying every minute doing the things I love best. I'm hoping you'll be able to steer me towards the best places to eat around here?"

"Oh yes, of course. We've got a good restaurant right in the village that specializes in local dishes. Their duck is incredible."

"I don't mean all fancy, by any means. I know back home,

sometimes the best food comes out of a broken-down shack, you know what I mean?"

"Lobster rolls," said Molly, getting misty-eyed for the first time over a memory from home.

Molly's cell rang and she saw it was Ben. "Excuse me, Eugenia, I need to take this." She got up and walked away from the table, guessing correctly that Ben might have news on the case.

Ben jumped right in without saying hello. "Whether Séverin did or didn't have an affair with Iris—doesn't matter anymore, he's got an alibi. Air-tight, three witnesses. He was working late and you know how exposed that office is. A number of people saw him there, sitting at his desk."

"Hm," said Molly. "And the witnesses cover all the time when the murder would have been possible?"

"I'm afraid so. It's been so hot, I guess a number of villagers were out stretching their legs that evening once it was a little cooler. And his office is extremely visible to anyone walking or driving down the street."

"Is one of those witnesses Caroline?"

"Yes, as a matter of fact. Why do you ask?"

"I'm interested in the way she keeps popping up to say that Séverin isn't guilty of anything. She claims he had no affairs even though village gossip and now his confession say otherwise. And now she provides him with an alibi for the night of the murder. Does this all fall under the heading of the duties of a very good assistant, or...or something else? And if he *was* seeing the woman she loved, why in the world would she be motivated to protect him? You'd think she'd be daydreaming about pushing *him* down a flight of stairs."

"I don't know, Molly," said Ben, a little distractedly. "I'm going over to see Pierre. The Lafonts told him he was not to come to work today as they wanted a day off from his hammering. I have a feeling the whole thing might finally hit him once he's home alone with nothing to distract him."

"You're a good friend."

"No. It's just what people do. Do me a favor, will you? Rustle up another suspect? I don't like how the field has narrowed again. I tried to float the idea of Caroline with Maron but I'm not sure if he'll bite."

"You think Caroline—?"

"It's possible. The thing is, I don't trust Maron to stick to the facts objectively. He's so desperate to get an arrest he's liable to try to shape the facts to fit whatever story he's come up with lately, and right now that means Pierre."

Molly sighed. "You never like admitting that someone from Castillac, someone you've known your whole life, could ever possibly be guilty of murder. Hasn't the last year put a dent in that fantasy?"

Ben didn't answer.

"I'm sorry, that sounded way harsher than I meant it. Only...be prepared, Ben, in case it *is* Pierre." She leaned down and picked an unfamiliar wildflower growing on the edge of the meadow. "I'm having breakfast with the new guest, and after that, I'm going to work in the garden and turn this whole thing over in my mind. I'll see if I can come up with any new avenues to pursue."

"Thanks, Molly," said Ben.

They hung up, both feeling a twinge of something they couldn't put their fingers on, but it wasn't happiness.

❧ 28 ❧

The next day, Ben and Molly met for breakfast once again at the Café de la Place. Molly loved sitting on the terrace on summer mornings when it seemed as though most of the village passed by. The air was the perfect temperature, and smells of coffee and fresh pastry filled the air.

Not to mention the dappled sun from plane trees, which she never got tired of looking at. The café was packed with people Molly had met: Rex Ford, an art teacher at L'Institut Degas; Madame Gervais, who had just had her 103rd birthday; and Nathalie Marchand, the pretty manager at the restaurant La Métairie. Molly went from table to table, kissing cheeks and exchanging greetings, and finally sat down at the table with Ben.

He leaned back in his chair, grinning at her. "You really fit in now," he said approvingly. "And your French—remember when you first got here, how you stumbled over everything?"

"I was horrible!" she said, grinning.

"And now you scamper about using the subjunctive as though you were born here." He paused. "I hope it won't sound too nitpicky to say that your genders remain a bit dicey."

Molly laughed. "Not nitpicky, just true. I hope eventually, by the time I'm Madame Gervais's age, most of it will have sunk in. In the meantime, I'm not worrying about it."

"I believe the English expression is 'other fish to cook'?"

"Fry," said Molly.

The weather was sparkling with exactly the right amount of warmth, her guests were a pleasure, she had a murder to solve and a handsome boyfriend to have breakfast with. All was right in Molly's world, for the moment, and she turned her face to the sun and closed her eyes, anticipating that first bite of croissant that she never tired of. And then her thoughts turned to the case.

"So how was Pierre yesterday?" she asked.

"Eh, it's hard to say. He lets no emotion out, even to me. He talked at great length about the staircase he's building, and also a bit about your barn."

"Ah, the barn. I hope he gets around to that project eventually. The pigeonnier, as I'm sure I've said fifty times—it's a masterpiece."

"Yes, well, we're going to have to keep him out of prison if he's to be making any other masterpieces. Maron had been focusing on Séverin but now he's back to Pierre. I'm not sure how sold he was on the idea that Caroline might have had some hand in this—and I'm not either, not necessarily anyway. That poem…I'm not entirely sure what to make of it. But in any case, as far as Pierre goes? We need a break, and fast."

Molly watched Pascal moving gracefully through the tables with their order on a tray. "There is pretty much no luxury I appreciate more than someone headed my way with food on a tray," she said.

Pascal kissed cheeks and hurried back to the kitchen; the Café was crowded and he had no time to chat.

"I take your silence to mean that you still have Pierre in your sights as the prime suspect?"

Molly considered, nibbling on the crispy end of her croissant. She had spent hours working in the front flower border the day before, mulling over every detail of the case but getting nowhere. "Well, who else is there that makes any sense? I don't think you can set aside the fact that Pierre hits a triple: means, motive and opportunity."

"Is that a football reference?"

"Baseball." Molly was trying to hold on to her sunny mood but it was drooping fast. Why was Ben being so pigheaded about Pierre? It's not like they were great friends. She wasn't sure Ben even liked him.

Ben's cell buzzed and he pulled it out of his pocket. "It's Maron," he said to Molly before taking the call.

"Bonjour Maron...yes...interesting. Anything else?....Bon." He ended the call and looked at Molly, chewing his lip in thought. "Curious," he said.

"What? Come on, what did he say?" Molly had to make an effort not to shout.

Ben lowered his voice. "He had Séverin's office computer brought in. Turns out it was loaded with emails to Iris."

"Figures."

"And the final one, dated the night of her murder, was a break-up email."

They both stared, thinking this over.

"So, alibi aside, our motive for Séverin doesn't check out either. Séverin didn't murder Iris in a rage when she broke it off with him. *He* broke up with *her*," said Ben.

"But...okay. Wait. Were there answers to any of them from Iris?"

"Yes. They had an email conversation that went on for several months, apparently. Until the night she died, when he ended it."

Molly was so agitated she stood up and walked to the sidewalk.

"Are you finished?" said Ben, incredulous, since Molly was not usually one to leave a half a croissant behind.

"No, I'm...I just need to move around while I think. I know

I've been ringing the Pierre bell since the very beginning, but maybe...maybe this whole thing is lot more complicated than it looks. And maybe you're right, the obvious solution isn't the correct one. We've got a lot more work to do, Ben, that's what just hit me. A *lot* more."

Ben only nodded and took a sip of his coffee.

"We keep making assumptions. To hear that Séverin broke up with Iris—do you see how we just assumed it was the other way around? That no man would ever break up with her because she was too good-looking? And the worst part is—we made the assumption without even realizing it. That is fatal to getting to the truth."

Dufort couldn't help smiling. "You're not an amateur at this anymore, you know that?"

Molly shook off the compliment. "Would you mind if I talked to Pierre by myself?" she asked.

"Not at all."

"All right. I think I'll start there." She ate up the rest of her croissant and was out of her chair again. "Excuse me for running off. Scooter's broken down so I have to walk everywhere, and I still don't have the right washers for that drippy sink in the pigeonnier, and good heavens I need to get back to La Baraque and give my neglected guests a little attention."

"Understood. See you later," said Ben. He reached for her hand, but she was already off down the sidewalk headed for the hardware store.

MOLLY WALKED HOME, almost the whole way worrying about how much the repair on the scooter was going to cost. The obvious thing to do was take it in for an estimate, but—and she knew perfectly well this was magical thinking of the most useless kind—if she put off going, she could keep hoping the problem was something cheap and easy to fix.

Once she turned in the driveway she could see that Roger Finsterman had set up his easel in the meadow again, and Molly went to ask his permission to go into the pigeonnier and work on the faucet.

"It's sort of a shame that I'm staying in the pigeonnier," said Finsterman as he squeezed some paint onto a well-used palette. "It's really a wonderful place, and I've barely spent any time in it. Been painting from the minute the sun's up until dark every day. So anyway—it's no problem, go ahead and do whatever work you need to. I'll probably take a break for lunch at around one, depending on how things are going. Usually I just get some bread and cheese and bring it outside."

"The weather has been perfection since that storm last week," said Molly. "Listen, excuse me if this is impolite...but would you mind if I took a look at what you're working on?"

"Not at all," answered Finsterman. "Though it's very unfinished."

Molly stepped around for a good view of the canvas. "Oh!" she said, before she could stop herself. The painting was the ugliest thing she had ever seen in her life. It was beyond ugly—looking at it actually made her feel queasy. She could not make out any relation to the meadow at all. "That...that is really something!" she said, trying to sound at least a little enthusiastic without utterly lying.

"It's not for everyone," said Finsterman, not fooled for an instant, and apparently not bothered.

Molly smiled and headed inside to the leaky faucet and got to work. Happily that particular repair went easily once she had the right size washer, and she was done in ten minutes—just in time to see Frances walking in the distance along rue des Chênes, about to turn into the driveway.

Leaving Finsterman to his work, she called Bobo and they

NELL GODDIN

went to greet her. Molly could tell by the way she walked that she was upset about something.

"What's wrong, Franny? Meet up with another bee?"

"If that was a joke, it's not funny," said Frances. She was wearing bicycle shorts, high-tops, and a T-shirt with holes in it, instead of her usual more sophisticated clothes.

"I wasn't joking. I can see something's wrong, what is it?"

"Can you make me a drink? Like, a real drink?"

"I've got some cold rosé, that's about it. My liquor cabinet is a little low at the moment."

"I don't care what the drink is, Molly, just get me one."

Molly's eyes widened. "At least you're not still smoking. What's wrong? Is it Nico? has he done something terrible?"

"No! Bite your tongue, Missy! Nico is...I love Nico, just to come right out with it. He's fantastic. But...."

Oh boy, thought Molly. All aboard the Frances Relationship Roller Coaster.

"...but what?"

"...but he's talking the M-word. And the C-word."

"Huh? Stop speaking in code and just come out with it. I don't know what those words *are*."

"*Marriage*, Molls! *Children!* And I...."

Her eyes now comically wide, Molly waited to hear what Frances was going to say.

"It's just, you know, with two divorces under my belt already, it seems like I should just accept that marriage and I don't go together very well. And children? I've honestly never really thought about it, not seriously. I know I'm verging on forty, but that nesting thing women talk about? Has never hit me."

Molly was speechless.

"And also...I know that having children is like your dream. This may be...I don't know...it's just that I'm having trouble figuring out what I think about Nico's proposal, partly because I think you'll be really upset with me and sad about it. If I marry him and start popping out the rugrats or something."

She took a slow breath. "Oh, Frances. I'm not part of this equation at all. Your life with Nico...it shouldn't be limited by anything I have or don't have in my life. That would be nuts. Truly." She put an arm around Frances and squeezed her.

"So you wouldn't be mad?"

Molly managed a smile. "Of course not. Will I feel a twinge if you two have a baby? Of course. I feel twinges at every baby that crosses my path. I had a good cry over Oscar the other night because I still miss him, and I only knew him for a few weeks. Please, Frances...do what's right for you and Nico."

"You are a good friend, Mollster."

"So...you're really happy with him?"

"I'm—yes. I am. Of course I doubt it, I wonder what-does-it-all mean. I think it can't possibly last: all the usual relationship pessimism, which I feel like I have a right to just because of my history."

"That Texas oilman was not really suited to you," said Molly, holding back a grin.

"Haha—Rex? He was an idiot. Fun, though. Really knew how to throw a party."

"And husband number 2?"

"Okay, well, Duane had the soul of a poet, he really did."

"I bet that got old."

"In about ten minutes, yeah."

"So...if you can...tell me what might you be saying about Nico in a few years? What's the quality that attracts you?"

Frances spoke quietly. "He's on my side, Molls."

Molly and Frances looked at each for a long time without saying anything, their eyes getting a little moist.

"That's pretty much it right there," Molly said. "So would you stay in Castillac? Please?"

"You know I'm a nomad at heart. But yeah, you managed to

find a real gem of a village. I love it here. Even though people do seem to get bumped off at an alarming rate."

The two friends stopped to pet Bobo on their way inside. Molly stood up and stretched, a little stiff from all the walking of the last few days.

"So..." said Frances, "you don't say much about you and Ben lately. Like, nary a word."

Molly bustled inside. "Come on in. I'll get you that glass of rosé if you still want it. And I found a cheese at the market you're not going to believe..."

Frances followed, but she noticed, as anyone would have, that Molly was sometimes a lot more enthusiastic about asking questions than she was about answering them.

❧ 29 ❧

The next morning Molly threw herself into cleaning the house to a standard far higher than usual. She was no slob, and so it was not very grungy before she began. But whenever she felt a certain kind of sadness, housecleaning was what she did.

Frances with a baby. Frances a mother?

By the time the living room, kitchen, and her bedroom were sparkling, the emotion had receded and Molly felt like seeing people—any people, really, just some talking and laughing and connection. Eugenia Perry had taken off to see Château Marainte and she didn't want to bother Finsterman. For the first time in what felt like a long time, she strolled over to see her neighbor, Madame Sabourin.

But she wasn't home.

She called Ben and got his voicemail. She sent some emails to friends back home, asking if anyone felt like skyping, but got no answer. What's an extrovert to do? she wondered with frustration.

Finally she had some lunch and then attacked the garden, accomplishing all kinds of cleanup chores she's been putting off, plus edging the front border, deadheading the roses, and putting some compost around the peonies. She mowed the grass, front and back of the house.

She lay down for an hour and read a mystery on her tablet, feeling envious at the way the clues all fell into place for the heroine. And then, thinking some more about the Gault case, she shut off her tablet and got up with renewed purpose. I'll go see Pierre, she thought. See if I can find out for sure whether he knew about his wife's affair.

It occurred to her that maybe she should take Frances with her, since she planned to ask some difficult questions and who knows how he might respond. He might get angry...or who knows, even violent. He was always so controlled...but what if the dam holding back all those feelings finally broke? She wasn't sure she wanted to be in the way.

Frances is too much of a wild card. Just her presence will get everything off the subject. I'll just be careful, and if he starts getting really upset, I'll leave.

She put on sneakers and set off down rue des Chênes, having given Bobo some stern words about following her.

I've got to think through everything logically, and not make any assumptions, she told herself. So let's see...maybe Pierre did not know what Iris was up to. Maybe he knew but did not care. Seems unlikely, and heaven knows I don't understand that—but for some people, it just isn't a big deal, and maybe Pierre is in that group. Maybe he was even having an affair of his own.

When she got to the cemetery, Molly glanced inside, then went through the iron gate with 'Priez pour vos Morts' inscribed overhead. It was around dinnertime and no one was there. Passing by the marble headstone for Joséphine Desrosiers, Molly kept going down that row and then turned up the third aisle beyond it where Iris was buried.

"Hello," Molly said impulsively. She felt foolish talking out loud to a dead person but continued nonetheless. "First of all, I'm really sorry we didn't have time to get to know each other. I had a feeling that night I met you that we would have been friends, maybe good friends. What happened to you...it was a terrible tragedy. I guess I don't need to point that out to you. But I mean a tragedy for all the people connected to you and also all the people who hadn't gotten a chance to know you yet.

"I don't have any idea why I'm standing here giving a speech in an empty cemetery. It's just...I guess what I want to say is...that I will do my best to find out who's responsible. I wish you could give me a little hint. What was it like? Did you see it coming?"

Molly squatted down beside Iris's grave. It did not have a headstone but instead a glossy flat piece of marble lying on top, almost like the cover of a book. The engraved inscription included only her name and dates, with a small flower underneath. Understated, and quite moving. Given Pierre's obsession with stone, Molly wondered if he had chiseled the inscription himself. He had seemed so distracted at the funeral, not in a frantic way but placidly so, as though he wasn't thinking about where he was or why but off on some daydream...but grief can look a lot of different ways, she reminded herself. Maybe he wasn't bored or thinking about work the way he seemed, but quite the opposite—so gutted he couldn't express it at all.

Maybe.

Molly gathered up a few pebbles from the path and put them on the edge of the gravestone, as a way to mark her visit, and to show that Iris was not forgotten.

THE GAULT HOUSE was on the edge of the village but on the opposite side from La Baraque, so it took some time to walk there. For once Molly did not notice the golden limestone of the old buildings, the sounds of villagers having quiet dinners, or the worn cobblestones as she walked down alleys. She walked right past the La Perla house which had a clothesline full of freshly washed underthings and didn't even see it. Instead she was thinking hard about everyone related to Iris's case, and trying to look at them from a different perspective than she had thus far managed to cultivate.

Caroline Dubois. Wild crush on Iris, obviously furious at and envious of Séverin. What's her romantic history like? Seems wound a little tight. Could she have gotten into a tussle with Iris out of frustration, and pushed her sort of by accident?

Tristan Séverin. Seems like a decent sort, likes kids. Was seeing Iris romantically, but has an alibi. Plus he broke up with Iris, not the other way around.

Pierre.

Pierre.

Who else haven't we considered? Iris seems to have inspired so much passion—perhaps someone else was obsessed with her, someone who kept his or her feelings secret? Or...could it have been someone more on the fringes of Iris's life—someone who did some work at their house, for instance, or even someone just passing through? Oh boy, when I get to considering the old murdering-sociopath-just-passing-through-town, I know I'm hitting a brick wall, she thought.

There was always the possibility that Iris hadn't been pushed at all. Nagrand said he thought she had been, but he couldn't say absolutely. But Molly wasn't willing to call it an accident since it felt like taking the easy way out, and could mean a killer would get off free.

It was dusk. Birds were twittering and the air was soft. She got to the Gault's driveway and walked towards the house, but when she didn't see Pierre's truck, she took the gravel path around to the garden. The roses were blooming in wild profusion, some of the flowers as big as bread plates, the reds deep and velvety.

Her rose obsession allowed her to identify a vigorous *Étoile de Hollande* climbing up a metal rose pillar. Red for love, she thought, cupping a bloom in her hands and leaning down to smell the heady aroma. The garden was starting to show signs of Iris's absence: weeds were sprouting up in the gravel path as well as the beds, and the whole place had a somber air of neglect. Molly disliked gardens that were too neat, but this wasn't a splendid messy abundance but instead the slow deterioration of the order Iris had designed for it. It made Molly feel suddenly and over-whelmingly sad, far more than she had in the cemetery.

She wandered along the path in the deepening darkness. How late did Pierre work, anyway? When he worked for her he had always stayed until the last ray of sun disappeared—not exactly rushing home to his beautiful wife, which Molly realized now she'd never given a thought to, but just been glad he was working so hard on her project.

Did Pierre work so much because his home life was unpleas-ant? Dull? Worse than dull? Or did he work because he loved it, and Iris was happy for him to do so?

So many questions. And the old cliché was true: nobody knows what goes on in a marriage except the people who are in it. And sometimes maybe not even them, she thought.

Molly couldn't help squatting down and pulling a few weeds out of a border of santolina and lavender that were ruining the pattern. For a few moments she was absorbed in the task, her mind more or less blank.

Then she heard something. Thinking it was Pierre, she stood up and looked around. It was dark. She didn't see lights from the truck, or anyone walking around the house. Nothing but trees swaying in the light breeze, and a rustling out in the woods that sounded like a squirrel.

Then she heard the noise again. It sounded like the sound of a hand clapping on a body, the sound of someone patting someone on the back with some vigor.

A prickle of fear ran up back of her neck. Was someone watching her from the shadows? And what on earth was he doing to make that sound?

She started walking towards the house while getting out her cell. She stopped to look around, about to call Ben, but instead kept going around the house, where she was surprised to see Pierre's truck now parked by the back door. She must have been so absorbed in her thoughts that she hadn't heard it pull into the driveway.

"Pierre?" she called out. There were no lights on in the house. Molly trotted up the steps to the front door and knocked but heard no sound from inside. She waited another few seconds, called again, and then hurried down the driveway and back into the village, feeling thoroughly spooked but also embarrassed since she hadn't even seen anyone. Why was Pierre's truck back, but no Pierre? Had he gone inside and wouldn't answer?

For someone in his predicament, he acted...weird. Molly realized that it made her angry at him—if he was innocent, then stop acting so guilty! Innocent people don't hide inside with the lights off not answering the door when a friend knocks!

Well, she thought, to be honest I'm not really Pierre's friend. A client is what I am to him. But still. The insurance money, his demeanor at the funeral and the whole time since the murder, the affair...every bit of circumstantial evidence was stacked against him. Yet because of the way Iris had died, there might never be a way to prove he did it.

She walked past Lapin's antique/junk shop, and then the lamp shop and Madame Gervais's house on rue Baudelaire. Oh, how she missed her scooter! Tomorrow morning she would take it to the shop for sure, no more excuses.

It felt like a long, lonely walk back to La Baraque, so she decided to stop by Chez Papa just in case anyone she knew was there. From a few blocks away she could see the twinkling lights Alphonse had strung on the spindly tree outside; the sight gladdened her heart and she broke into a jog to get there as soon as she possibly could.

"Molly!" called Nico as she came through the open door. The usual crowd was there: Lawrence, dressed impeccably, perched on his stool, Negroni in place. Frances sat next to him with a pile of napkins on the bar in front of her, Lapin on her other side with a beer.

"Bonsoir *à tous!*" she said, trying to sound jolly. The brisk walk had dissipated some of the creepy feeling but she was still a little rattled. "Looks like a full house tonight. What's the occasion?"

"Don't know of any," said Nico.

"Every table in the back room is filled," said Lawrence. "Here, take my stool. I'd say let's move to a table but there aren't any left."

"I would never steal your throne," said Molly, grinning. "Nico?"

"On it," said Nico, picking up the bottle of crème de cassis for Molly's kir.

She looked around at the crowd and immediately perked up, seeing Caroline Dubois sitting at a table with another woman Molly hadn't seen before. And farther down the bar, she thought she saw the handyman from the school, though she wasn't absolutely positive it was him.

"Hey Lapin," she whispered. "The guy down at the other end of the bar. No, the other end. Do you know him?"

"That's Hector Peletier," said Lapin in a loud voice.

"Shh!" hissed Molly. "You didn't have to announce it to the world!"

Lapin shrugged and drank his beer. "I must say, Molly, summer is my favorite season now that you've moved to Castillac." He ran his eyes up and down her body and waggled his eyebrows.

"Oh, shut up, Lapin," said Molly, glad that at least she had changed out of the tight camisole she had been wearing earlier, into a loose shirt with no sleeves. "So—and please keep your voice down—what do you know about him?"

"Eh, what do you want to know? He's a little younger than me so I wasn't in school with him. He's got a lot of brothers and sisters. One of them got in some trouble for selling marijuana a few years ago."

"Who are his friends? Do you know what he does with himself when he's off work?"

"You'd have to ask him," said Lapin. "I like it better when you talk about me," he said under his breath.

Turning to Frances, Molly said "What's up?"and gave her friend a light poke to get her attention.

"Oh, mon Dieu. Deadline. I need to deliver a jingle in two days and I'm nowhere. Something's really messing with my mojo. Every time I think I've got a good idea, it fizzles up in smoke."

"Have another drink," offered Lapin.

"I only drink lemonade when I'm working," she said, without looking up, continuing to doodle on a napkin. Nico reached under the bar for the lemons and started making it for her.

"Want to come over and use my piano?" asked Molly.

"Yeah, sure. But I can't even get to the stage in the process where I need the piano. I need to have at least the germ of an idea first…"

Molly wanted to ask whether she had decided to marry Nico, but of course that would have to wait until they were alone together. Now that Frances and Nico had gotten serious, Molly saw a lot less of her friend, and there was something quite different about her. Maybe…might it be…*happiness?*

"Lawrence, you're awfully quiet."

"Yes. Well. Just between you and me, my dear…lately I've been in rather a slough of despond."

"Oh my. What's it about?"

"Oh…I was going to say I don't know, but in fact, I do. It's my birthday coming up. I usually don't give birthdays much of a thought, really. You know—or maybe you're not quite old enough —at a certain point, they all start to run together, and I swear I have to do the math to figure out how old I am. So I'm a bit surprised it's hitting me so hard."

"So how decrepit are you?"

"On the 4th of August I'll be fifty-seven years old. Fifty seven!"

"One foot in the grave," said Lapin merrily.

"Shall we have a party?" asked Molly. "Maybe if we embrace it, it won't sting so much?"

Lawrence's expression softened. "A party would be lovely, dearest Molly."

"Disco theme," piped up Frances.

"Perfect! I bet I can get a glitter-ball from somewhere. And we can get all the music online. Donna Summer, the Bee Gees…."

Lawrence was laughing. "I might have a white suit tucked away somewhere, though it's more of a loose linen suit, not like Travolta's…"

"No, loose linen won't do. Frances will get you outfitted, right?" Frances nodded. "She used to do costumes for all the shows, back in the day. She's genius at it."

"You're saying she'll be able to find me a 70s disco suit in Castillac?"

"I may have to cast a wider net than the village," said Frances. "Just leave it to me." She clapped her hands. "Oh, I'm so pleased to have a project other than this stupid jingle! Let's drink to procrastination!"

Everyone at the bar raised their glasses and clinked. "To procrastination!"

Molly peeked out of the corner of her eye at Caroline Dubois, who had pulled her chair right up close to the woman she was having dinner with. "Hey Lawrence," she said, sotto voce, "do you know her? The woman in the navy jacket?"

"No, but I admire the jacket. It looks perfect on her, for one thing. Beautiful cut, though I'd imagine it might be a little warm this time of year."

Molly nodded, thinking.

"Does this have something to do with Iris?"

Molly nodded again. There she was with Hector on one side and Caroline on the other, but how to approach them?

Did they both have a thing for Iris? Did either of them know something they weren't telling?

"I'm gonna...I'll be back in a minute," she murmured, and walked over to Caroline's table. "Bonsoir, Caroline," she said warmly. "It's so packed in here tonight, huh?"

Caroline met Molly's gaze but did not smile. She put her arm around the woman she was with, her fingers stroking her bare shoulder.

"Sorry, am I interrupting?" Molly took a step backwards.

"It's all right. Do you know each other? Molly Sutton, let me present my friend Kath Halliwell."

"Nice to meet you," said Molly, who couldn't help noticing that Kath might have had one too many drinks. Her eyes were glassy as she smiled at Molly without speaking. "Can I join you just for a moment?" she asked, sliding into a chair despite Caroline's chilliness.

"Did you know Iris too?" Molly asked Kath.

"How dare you," said Caroline in a low voice. "Do you run around the village like a vulture, picking over the bones of everyone who dies? Is that what you do?"

Molly sat up very straight. "I'm sorry? I don't understand why you're angry with me. Don't you want us to find out what happened to Iris?"

"You're just interested in getting another notch on your belt. 'Look at me, everyone, I come barging in from America and start solving all the mysteries in the département!' You don't care about Iris. It doesn't even matter to you if you get it right—as long as you can get someone arrested and bask in the glory, that's good enough, right?"

"What? Caroline, you've really got me all wrong—"

"I don't think so, Madame Sutton. You come over here and sit down without being invited, thinking you'll catch me in some little lie, and pin Iris's murder on me. That's what you're up to, isn't it?"

Even though Caroline was not at all topping out Molly's list of suspects, the grain of truth in what Caroline said made Molly pause.

"You think because I'm gay, I'm capable of anything, is that it?"

At that Molly burst out with a laugh. "Caroline, I don't know what's given you these wrong ideas about me, but I will tell you, they are dead wrong!"

"See, you can't get a sentence out without saying 'dead'. You're like a circling hyena, scavenging on Castillac."

Finally the penny dropped and Molly realized Caroline as well as Kath had had too much to drink. She hadn't seemed that tipsy at first. Kath, who didn't appear to be taking in any of the conversation, slumped her head on Caroline's shoulder.

"Look, I'm sorry to have interrupted. You have a good night," said Molly, heading to the bathroom in the back of the bar. She splashed some water on her face and looked in the mirror, wondering what Caroline saw when she looked at her. A homophobic vulture-hyena, apparently.

By the time she rejoined her friends, everyone was beginning to drift home. She hugged Frances and asked her to come over in the morning, kissed Lawrence goodnight and made a plan to get together later in the week, and waved at Nico as she left to walk home.

The night had been a failure in every direction. Pierre in hiding, no useful information on Hector, an accusatory Caroline.

Maybe this time, Molly was not going to get to the bottom of what happened. Maybe nobody ever would.

❧ 31 ❧

Molly got home from Chez Papa exhausted. It was far earlier than her usual bedtime but she fell gratefully into bed and fast asleep, so that when the sirens went past la Baraque they woke her out of a deep slumber. At first she thought she was back in Boston where sirens were commonplace; she nearly rolled over and went back to sleep. But as consciousness developed and she grasped that she was in a place where sirens hardly ever blared, she bolted out of bed and texted Lawrence, who so often seemed to know what was happening almost before it happened.

"No idea," he texted back.

It was not yet midnight. She texted Ben; he didn't know what had got the gendarmes out either. Molly couldn't help wishing sometimes that he was still Chief, with all the inside information and authority that came with the position. But that was over and done, he was happier now, and she'd have to find another way to get information. If she'd had the scooter, she might have ridden down the road to see for herself, but walking didn't seem like the best idea since she had no idea how far away the trouble was.

Now she was up, wide awake, and the wheels started turning.

Somewhere, somehow—I'm making a faulty assumption, she thought. I'm believing someone who is lying, making a connection where there is none, seeing something that isn't there. But *what?*

She poured herself the dregs of a bottle of rosé and went out to the dark terrace. Bobo roused herself to follow, and the orange cat showed up and rubbed against her ankles. Molly sipped the wine and looked up into the starry sky, thinking about Iris. Were you happy? she wondered. Did you ever believe anyone really loved you, and wasn't only carried away by your looks?

For what seemed like the thousandth time, Molly thought about everyone who had talked to her about Iris. She reviewed their conversations as best as she could, trying to listen more carefully, more objectively; to see if she could find the soft spot, the place in her thinking that was rotten.

Eventually she went back to bed, still wondering about the siren and what the trouble was, and slept only fitfully, restless enough that Bobo finally hopped out of her bed and went to sleep on the floor where it was peaceful.

❧ 32 ❧

Ilene Lafont was anxious to have the work on the addition finished, as homeowners in that situation understandably always are. She found it stressful making conversation with Pierre, hearing the sharp noise of metal on stone for hours on end, and her yard reduced to a construction site full of rubble for what seemed an eternity.

After dinner with her husband, Ilene finished her brandy and got a flashlight so she could go see what progress Pierre had made now that he was finally gone for the day. She saw that his truck had made a bad rut in the soft ground beside the driveway, and made a mental note to talk to him about that in the morning. Oh, she was going to be so happy to see these piles of stones gone and the gorgeous new addition finished!

The exterior walls of the addition did look beautiful. She ran the beam of the flashlight over them, admiring the way Pierre had managed to keep the feeling of centuries-old stonework while building something entirely new. The golden stone, the mortar, the placement of each stone...every detail was amazing...but it was inside, on the difficult staircase, where Pierre had been working that day, that she was most curious to see.

She pushed open the door and walked in. Her eyes went straight to the figure sprawled out on the floor at the bottom of the stairs. It was Pierre, his body crumpled unnaturally, not moving.

Ilene hesitated, then ran over to him. She was too rattled to think clearly—she put her hand over his heart to see if it was beating, then snatched her hand back and ran for the house, shouting for her husband.

About ten minutes later, as the Lafonts stood in the yard in a state of shock, they heard the siren, and less than a minute after that, Officer Monsour pulled into their driveway.

"A body?" he said, with no greeting or introduction."Where is it?"

"This way," said Victor. Ilene stayed behind, wringing her hands. She hadn't liked Pierre, not at all, and now she felt overwhelmed with guilt, even though she knew one thing had nothing to do with the other. It's not as if *she* had pushed him off the ladder after all.

"Pierre Gault, you say?"

"Yes."

"Husband of—"

"Yes. Of Iris. Both of them died by falling—it's too bizarre." Victor took out a handkerchief and wiped his clammy brow.

"When did you last see him alive?" Monsour asked.

"When I got home from work. It was right around five. He's been working here for quite a while, several months—it's a big project. Generally I would come over first thing when I got home, to see how things were coming along."

"And tonight how did he seem? Anything different? The least unusual?"

"No," answered Victor.

"Not upset, or worried about anything that you know of?"

"Not at all. Though as you say, his wife died last week. He never spoke of it to me. I expected him to take some time off but he refused, said coming to work was actually helpful—he never said a word more than he had to. We didn't...we didn't have the kind of relationship where you talk about that sort of thing. He'd tell me about the work he'd been doing that day, sometimes ask a question or two to clarify how we wanted the thing done. That was it, really. Strictly professional."

Monsour stroked his chin. It looked to him as though the man had taken a header off the ladder. Could have been an accident. Or he could have been pushed, or had the ladder yanked out from under him.

"And was it you who had these conversations with Monsieur Gault, not your wife?"

"That's right. My wife, she struggles to make small talk, and Pierre as well. So together..." Victor shrugged.

Monsour pulled out his cell and turned aside. First he called Florian Nagrand, the coroner, followed by Maron.

"Yes, the Lafont's. Route de Tournesol, it's just past...all right, I know you've lived here longer than I...pardon, Chief. Yes, I can affirm that he is dead...I do have some training, sir...all right. Yes... goodbye." With exasperation Monsour shoved his cell in its holster on his belt. He walked back to Pierre and squatted down. Pierre's wrist was bent back and Monsour had a strong urge to straighten it out, but knew not to touch anything until Nagrand had given him the okay.

"Does it seem to you that there are more murders in the village than is absolutely normal?" asked Victor, looking through the window hoping to see the coroner's car.

"Can't do much in the way of prevention," answered Monsour. "We generally only get the call after the fact."

"I wasn't trying to affix blame, merely wondering—"

"Do you have any reason to suspect foul play?" asked Monsour, pleased to be able to use the expression. "Have you seen anyone else on your property today?"

Victor shook his head. Monsour heard Maron's scooter in the

distance and went back outside. Victor followed, not wanting to be in the room alone with a dead man even for a second. He wondered whether he would have to pay Pierre's estate what he still owed, since the mason had no family—and then was appalled by having such an ungenerous thought when the man's body was still warm and lying right there in his own house.

"Do you need to ask me anything else?" he asked Monsour. "Can I go check on my wife? She's had quite a shock."

Monsour told Lafont to be back in five minutes because Maron would want to question him himself.

"Pierre Gault, really?" Maron said in a low voice as the two gendarmes walked back to the addition.

"Yes. I'm interested to hear what you think once you see him." Monsour was trying out a new strategy to deal with his boss: flattery mixed with a chumminess meant to warm him up a little.

Maron shot him a look, not fooled for a minute by Monsour's change in demeanor. "You called Nagrand? Where the hell is he? And Monsour, don't use the siren unless you have a reason. It's upsetting to the community and makes you look self-important."

Monsour blinked, not quite able to take in that his new strategy was off to such a terrible start.

Maron did not like hanging around dead bodies either. He knelt down beside Pierre, checking for a pulse in his neck just to be sure. "First the wife, then the husband. Well, there goes our prime suspect."

A scruffy terrier came sailing through the door and barked at the two men. "Get him out of here and shut the door," barked Maron. "I think I hear Nagrand, I'm going to check." A little lame for an excuse, but he felt like one more minute in the same room as Pierre and he might lose his dinner, and it had been a very good dinner indeed.

Maron stood looking around the Lafont's yard. It looked more or less like any construction site: ruts from truck tires, piles of stones on tarps, an upturned wheelbarrow, a pile of lumber. It was neater than usual, however, which didn't surprise Maron given that the Gault house and garden were so well-kept as to remind him of a movie set and not a place where people actually lived.

On his own the terrier shot back outside and Monsour slammed the door after him. Maron strode up to the main house and knocked, wanting Madame Lafont to go through her movements during the evening so that he could fix the time of discovery while it was still fresh in her mind, but before anyone came to the door Florian Nagrand turned into the driveway in his white work van.

"I was right at a very exciting part in the book I'm reading," groused Nagrand in his rough voice as he climbed out of the van. "My wife is not happy with you," he added.

"It's hardly my fault," said Maron. "This way. Did Monsour tell you—it's Pierre Gault. He was building this addition for the Lafonts. Nice job he was doing, eh?"

"He's a very good mason," said Nagrand. "Or was." He opened the door to the extension and looked at Pierre from a distance before going closer. Then he squatted down beside the body, not touching Pierre at first but looking at his position, and taking a few snaps with the camera on his phone.

"We're lucky it's not messier," he muttered.

"He's still warm, but that could simply be the fact that the air temperature is also quite warm for this time of night," said Monsour.

Nagrand sighed. Would the gendarmes never learn to let him do his job without always having to get their two cents in?

"Not to push you, Florian," said Maron. "But what do you think...an accident? Just fell off the ladder? Any possibility it could be suicide?"

"What would be most helpful is if you and Monsour would go out to the yard and see if you can find any evidence of anyone else visiting the Lafont's. Talk to them. Look for, I don't know, tire tracks or fallen buttons or whatever it is you look for. Where's Pierre's truck, by the way?"

Maron got a sick feeling in his stomach. The most obvious question in the world, and it took the coroner to ask it.

❦ 33 ❦

It was awkward, walking the scooter any long distance, and the mechanic's shop was on the other side of the village so that Molly's arm was aching from having to stretch across and guide the handlebars. Her mood was foul from frustration and not enough sleep, and she muttered under her breath as she made her way along.

When she was bumping down the alley next to the La Perla house, she stopped for a moment to rest her arm. Peeking over the wall, she saw that the clothesline was bare for once, with no fantastically expensive underwear dancing in the slight breeze, and no one in any of the backyards. The heat had started to build again and any villagers who weren't at work were sticking to the shade.

Just as an exercise, she considered the clothesline of the La Perla house and tried to come up with every possible assumption she could to explain why it was vacant that day. First—there was no fancy underwear on the line because it wasn't wash day. That was most likely the correct assumption, but, she reminded herself, most likely was not the same as true.

The La Perla woman could have moved.

She could have broken up with the husband or boyfriend who had given her the underwear, and thrown it all out in an attempt to erase bad memories.

She could have decided to switch brands.

She could have decided to go commando and forgo underwear altogether.

Okay, that last one was pretty unlikely...but this was only an exercise after all, and it was useful to remind herself that unlikely was still possible. Molly knocked back the kickstand of the scooter with her foot and kept trudging to the mechanic's.

"Bonjour!" she called out when she got there, seeing no one around. No answer. It was too early for lunch, the door to the garage was open, but no one was inside. She parked the scooter and went to wander around the village for a little while, planning to check back in a little later, having learned that sometimes in France, business was not the first thing on people's minds, but the proprietors might drift back to the shop at some point.

The village was quiet that morning with not a soul on the street. Molly thought about calling Ben, but...the truth was, she just didn't feel like it. She was disappointed in him for not accomplishing much of anything with the investigation except to defend Pierre at every turn. If Pierre was as innocent as he claimed, what evidence had he found to support it?

She had thought at first that any strong relationship should be able to weather a difference of opinion without too much trouble. Well, she still believed that, but was no longer so sure she and Ben were in that category.

However—this was not the day to think about that. She had to get the scooter fixed and talk to Nugent, that was all. Ben would have to wait.

Molly thought about going to see Madame Tessier, who almost always had a nugget or two of news, but what she was most in the mood for was hanging out with children. Any children, really, though she realized that some people might think she sounded like some kind of weirdo predator. It was only that her head had been filled with little but Iris for so long—with death and loss and sorrow—and she wished to hear the bubbling, innocent laughter of kids. Wanted to listen to rambling stories with no punchline, and be asked questions she had no idea how to answer.

In short, she missed Oscar and Gilbert and every other kid she'd gotten to know and love…but Oscar was in Australia and she knew Madame Gilbert was not her biggest fan.

Well, Pâtisserie Bujold would have to do.

§.

THE SHOP WAS empty except for Nugent.

"This heat, it's terrible for business," he groused, not giving Molly's chest so much as a sideways glance.

"It *is* hotter than I remember from last year," said Molly sympathetically.

"It is not good for the pastries, either."

"I expect not."

A long silence while Molly inspected the contents of the display case. Something about Nugent seemed off. Usually he stood behind the counter smiling in expectation of compliments, enjoying the way Molly looked over the day's selection. She kept glancing at him as she admired the row of strawberry tarts, next to a stately line of Napoleons, then cream puffs, pistachio *Jésuits*, buttery *palmiers*. He was paying no attention at all, but staring out of the window, his mouth drawn down at the corners.

Molly inhaled deeply, never tiring of the heady combination of butter and vanilla that was the hallmark of Pâtisserie Bujold. "So Edmond, I have to admit I haven't practiced making croissants even once. I don't know where I got the idea that moving to France would turn me practically into a woman of leisure with time for hobbies, because I'm quite busy, not that that's any excuse really."

Nugent turned his face towards Molly when she began speaking but did not change his expression. She waited for criticism, remonstration, at the very least some teasing…but Nugent said nothing.

"Would you be up for another lesson?" she blurted out, not remotely having intended to suggest such a thing.

Nugent startled. "Another lesson?"

"Yes. Maybe we could set aside croissants for the moment, give me a chance to practice that at home, and move on to something else? Éclairs, maybe? Are they very difficult?"

"Pssh," said Nugent with a wave of his hand. "A child could make them. Of course, the other *pâtissiers* in Castillac—their éclairs taste like cardboard. The shell is tough and overly chewy, the filling tastes like paste. So perhaps I should not insult children in this way."

Molly grinned, seeing him return to his old self a bit. "Excuse me if I'm being too pushy, but maybe…maybe we could do it right now, since the whole village seems to be hiding inside out of the heat? I guess the tourists are all looking for swimming pools instead of pastry. Anyway—what do you think?"

Nugent considered. Again Molly noticed that at no point did he look at her with his usual lasciviousness, which was certainly a relief…but what did it mean? And since when had he ever been reluctant to spend time alone with her?

"Actually Madame Sut—er, Molly. I'm not…it's been tough lately, I mean to say…."

Molly waited. She watched him grimace, saw his fists tighten. What is going on with him, she wondered.

"Oh, all right," he said finally. "Get your apron over there."

Molly put down her handbag and got the apron wrapped and tied around her. "Is something…is there anything you want to talk about?" she asked.

Nugent was getting a large bowl and a carton of eggs. "No.

No, I don't want to talk about it. Talking isn't going to bring her back, is it?"

"Iris?"

"Of course Iris! Who else would I be speaking of?"

Molly smoothed her palms over her apron, observing him.

"It's just—people don't understand. They don't *know*."

"Know what?"

Nugent appeared to be struggling. Molly was confused but felt there was something dangling in front of her to grab onto, a thread, a trail, but she couldn't quite see what it was.

"You didn't know her, Molly. We shared something, Iris and I. She came in almost every morning, always at the same time, right after I opened the shop at seven. She was an early riser, you see, just like me. About nine months a year she would be up at dawn to garden before she went to work, and she would come here to get a croissant or a roll, hot out of the oven. Iris knew my schedule intimately. She knew which days I made *tart tatin*. She knew that a *pain de campagne* has a thick crust to make it last longer.

"She paid *attention*, is what I am trying to impress upon you. We...we had something, Iris and I." Nugent drew in a long, snuffly breath. He opened his hands and closed them again tightly, then banged them on the counter. "That Pierre, he is nothing but a brute. Hardly deserving of her. Séverin—he's much younger than I, all right, I have eyes in my head. It's not an utter mystery to me why she might have chosen him. But he didn't *esteem* her, not like I did. No. He broke up with her, didn't he? Just tossed her aside when he was done like she was nothing more than an empty beer bottle."

Nugent put his hands over his face and Molly thought she heard a sniffle.

"I'm so sorry," she said. "I only met her that one time but I got the instant feeling we were going to be friends."

"And doubtless you would have been." Nugent's shoulders

drooped. "Get out a big bowl. Sift the flour. Take out a saucepan and the milk."

Molly moved around the kitchen at Nugent's bidding, her mind only half on what she was doing. She had milk heating up and the flour and salt sifted when her cell whistled.

"You mind if I get that?"

Nugent waved his hand in the air to say he didn't care and then leaned heavily on the counter while Molly rummaged through her bag.

It was a text from Frances.

Pierre dead.

"What?" Molly said out loud.

"Is something the matter?" asked Nugent, hearing the shock in Molly's tone.

Molly was furiously tapping more questions to Frances. "I just heard—something about Pierre. Hold on, I'm trying to get more details."

Nugent turned away. His jaw was set and he did not smile, though Molly might have detected an expression of satisfaction on his face if she had been able to see it.

❦ 34 ❦

Molly cut short the lesson on éclairs, which Nugent barely seemed to notice. She ran back down rue Picasso to see if the mechanics had shown up, and found her scooter parked outside with a ticket attached to the handlebars. It had been cleaned up and the brown paint shone as much as such a muddy color could. She pushed open the door and said hello.

"Ah, Madame Sutton! We saw that you left your scooter here and figured there was some kind of problem, so we went ahead and took a look at it. You'll be happy to hear it needed only a minor adjustment to the carburetor. I fixed it up and you're all set to go."

"What?" Molly was having a hard time taking in the good news right on top of the shocking news about Pierre. "I'm set to go?"

"Not to be a nag, but you might take a little better care of her," said the mechanic. Wipe off some of the mud every once in a while."

"You mean...it's running now?"

"Purring like a kitten," said the mechanic with a small smile.

Molly thanked him, and thanked him profusely when he told her she owed him nothing. No parts, and it had only taken him five minutes. But she made no move to leave, instead stood there staring at a truck in the parking lot, thinking.

"Do you mind if I ask a question? How hard would it be to…to make a truck start without a key?" she asked, not knowing the French word for hotwire.

"Are you planning a new career in vehicle theft? You know the French system would make it next to impossible for you to find a buyer. Or are you going to forge paperwork to go with it?" The mechanic was chuckling now, enjoying this idea of Madame Sutton, master criminal.

"What I'm wondering about is…well, did you know Pierre Gault? Have you heard what happened?"

"Of course I know Pierre. I saw him just yesterday. He brought the truck in for an oil change."

"Wait, what?"

The mechanic shrugged. "Of course he could do it himself easily enough. But if you know Pierre, you know all he cares about is stones! He's got rocks in head!" He laughed. "So I take care of his truck for him."

"So you changed the oil, and then he came and picked it up? This was yesterday?"

"No, not—sometimes that's how we do it. This time he's working out on route de Tournesol and it's too far for him to walk. So after we changed the oil, the easiest thing was for me to drive the truck over to his place—it's not far from here—and leave it for him. He said he'd get a ride home from the guy he's doing the work for."

So no wonder Pierre hadn't answered when she knocked on his door last night, she thought. Well, that's one mystery solved, though not the one I'd have chosen. Still, baby steps….

Molly said, "I'm sorry to be the one to tell you, but apparently Pierre…he fell off a ladder at the worksite. Didn't survive the fall."

The mechanic stared at her. "He's...?"

Molly nodded. She searched for something to say, some explanation, some comfort, but could find nothing. She grasped hands with the mechanic and the two of them held on tight, their eyes getting damp, shaking their heads in unison.

THE SCOOTER *WAS* PURRING like a kitten, though Molly could hardly enjoy it as she rode distractedly back to La Baraque. She kept seeing this image in her mind, over and over, of the stolid Pierre toppling off a ladder and falling onto what was likely a stone floor. Ugh. She had seen him on ladders many days at La Baraque, as he shaped the walls of the pigeonnier, and it had seemed to her at the time that he was terrifically nimble, much more so than one would have expected given his heavy body type. He had scrambled up and down ladders and on the roof of the building like a ten year-old in a tree, as physically capable as anyone you could imagine.

She couldn't help wondering: had he fallen? Or was the truth more complicated than that?

No matter what, Ben was going to be devastated. Molly wanted to check on Eugenia and begin planning Lawrence's birthday party, but first, after a calming few minutes petting Bobo, she settled on the terrace in the shade and called him.

"I've been trying to reach you," he said flatly.

"You have? Maybe I had the ringer off by mistake—so sorry but I've been running around the village and just got home. Ben, I'm heartbroken about Pierre."

"Really? That's something of a surprise."

Molly drew in a long breath. She knew better than to get into an argument now, when the news was so fresh. "Do you think it was an accident?" she asked quietly.

"I do not."

Molly waited but Ben did not elaborate. She wanted to know if he'd been in touch with Maron and Monsour but of course Ben knew that perfectly well and was choosing not to say. "Would you like to come over?" she asked.

"I have work to do." His tone was rough and Molly's eyes widened at the chilliness of it. "I'll call later," he added, more softly, and they hung up.

Well.

I'm not going to think about that right now, she said to herself, jumping up and getting a pad and pen. Instead I'm going to figure out the guest list for Lawrence's birthday and work on the menu, then call Frances to see if she'll help.

Castillac was going to have its first American disco 70s party, and there was no reason in the world Molly couldn't arrange that with one hand and work on the Iris case on the other. It might be the only way to save things between her and Ben.

Though if that's true, what we have is just not that solid, is it?

Not thinking about that right now.

She called Frances. "So if we have music and dancing, we're not going to want a heavy meal," she said. Often she and Frances talked to each on the phone like this—dispensing with greetings and picking up a conversation where it had been left off even if it was days before.

"Correct," answered Frances. She was lying on the sofa at Nico's with her long legs up over the back of it, sweating because the windows were closed to keep any stray bees from flying in. "Although one thing I've learned from Nico—the French do not play fast and loose with meals the way we do. You're not going to be able to serve cocktails and potato chips and call it a night."

"Now in what universe would I ever have done something like that?"

"Just saying."

"Finger food or sit-down with plates?"

"How many people are you having?"

"Oh, right. I should really do that first." There was a long pause as Molly thought. "You know, I just had a little idea."

"Uh huh. You've always just had a little a little idea. What is it this time?"

"I think I'll keep it to myself for now. But the guest list—it's going to be on the large side." Molly let out a cackle. "And if things work out the way I want them to, this party is going to be *epic.*"

❦ 35 ❦

The next few days went by in a whirlwind of studying recipes, searching for ingredients, and calling to invite a long list of people. Molly needed Constance to come in the day of the party to do some desperately needed cleaning.

"Constance, is there any way you can rearrange your schedule? I'm having almost thirty people over and my living room is covered with dog hair!"

"It's just that Thomas and I—"

"And of course you're both invited! The reason I'd like you to clean on Thursday is that if you do it earlier, it'll be a wreck again before the party. I'll do all the kitchen clean-up myself. And maybe I can get Frances to help you."

"The last time you tried that, all she did was dance around with the broom singing songs from Gene Kelly movies."

"You don't like Gene Kelly? I'd have thought you were too young to know who he is."

"Molls! Just because I'm not as old and decrepit as some people doesn't mean my life has been a cultural wasteland."

Molly sighed and laughed at the same time.

"Plus if you want me to do what you're asking, insulting me is not the way to get there."

"Constance, no insult intended, I promise. Please? I'll make it up to you somehow. This is not just any party. It's…it's important."

"Yeah yeah, I know, Lawrence is your bestie. All right, I'll talk to Thomas. He made the plans so I'm not going to cancel without talking to him first."

"Understood! Thanks a billion!"

"Um hm," said Constance, sounding huffy but actually enjoying the whole conversation immensely.

"All right then, see you Thursday morning unless I hear otherwise?"

Constance agreed and they hung up. Molly consulted her list, which at this point was two pages of illegible scratchings with items checked off and scribbled notes in the margins and other things crossed out. The menu was ambitious: lavender spritzers, toasted slices of baguette spread with goat cheese and *duxelles*, camembert and fig tartines, frisée salad with *lardons* and a mustard dressing, *ratatouille*, duck *confit*, and *profiteroles* covered in birthday candles for dessert. And this time she wasn't going to forget the ingredients for Lawrence's obligatory Negronis.

She had held her breath when calling a few people, but so far everyone had agreed to come. Eugenia graciously offered to help in the kitchen, saying that people from Louisiana have an affinity for French food and there was far too much to do for one cook.

"Well, I'm not making the duck confit from scratch," Molly said to her when they were having a planning meeting.

"Good thing—it takes days, doesn't it?"

"Yes. So I'm just buying them from the specialty food shop in town. They suggested catering the whole business, and I was tempted…but I didn't even ask how much that would cost. I'm being financially irresponsible enough as it is."

"But it's your best pal's birthday. What better occasion to splurge?"

"My thoughts exactly," said Molly. "Now what do you think about a dance floor? I hate to say it but I almost picked up the phone to call Pierre, the mason who died a few days ago, to ask him how hard would it be to make one."

Eugenia shook her head. "He's the man who did the work on the pigeonnier?"

"Yes. Very talented."

"I'll say. But...to go back to the dance floor, I think it'll be just fine to dance in the yard. Cut the grass real low to define the area, put on some Donna Summer, and people will hop to it."

"Do you think people here will even know who Donna Summer is? Or anyone younger than me? I was just a little kid when disco was a thing. Once I grew up a little and discovered the blues, that's all I ever listened to."

"The blues? Girl, you have *got* to come visit me in Louisiana. I can take you to hear music you will not believe."

"You're on. Okay, what do you think about seating? Shall we do one long table in the yard, with a white tablecloth and lots of candles?"

"Yes ma'am, you should. Do you have enough tables? Want me to figure that out?"

Molly grinned. "You don't speak French, Eugenia, or know a single soul in the village. How are you going to borrow enough tables for thirty people?"

Eugenia waggled her eyebrows. "You underestimate me, darlin'. Cross that off your list—I'll get it done."

The work of getting ready for the party was almost enough to put both the shaky state of things with Ben and the murder of Iris Gault out of Molly's mind. Almost, but not quite.

Molly was thrilled to celebrate Lawrence's birthday, hoping it would help to drag him up out of the 'slough of despond', as he put it. But that wasn't all she was hoping to accomplish.

She had another plan. Sort of.

❦ 36 ❦

By Thursday morning, the day of, Molly was exhausted. She and Eugenia had spent the day before cooking everything they could in advance, which necessitated a massive clean-up in the kitchen and left the refrigerator stuffed to the gills. She had made several emergency trips into the village for supplies and ingredients, and had to borrow Nico's car at one point to drive into Périgueux for a few things she couldn't get in Castillac. Because as anyone will tell you, you cannot have a 70s disco party without a glitter-ball to light up the dance floor.

But nevertheless, so far everything was going fairly smoothly. Frances reported that she had gotten perfect outfits for them, including Lawrence, and Constance had shown up on time and gone about her tasks in her usual cheerful and inefficient way.

"I know I sound fussy, but Constance, you're going to have to bring the vacuum back over here and vacuum the sofa cushions."

"Are you putting your shoes up on the sofa, you heathen?" shot back Constance.

"No! It's Bobo. She knows perfectly well she's not allowed on the sofa, but she sneaks in here when I'm asleep and you see the result. I'm sure the dog and cat owners of the party will be mostly understanding, but the others will be horrified."

"Well, the vac is not going to get that up. Lucky for you I brought my magic brush." She went to her bag sitting on the floor of the foyer and brought out a nondescript plastic brush with a sort of velvety pad on it. She swiped it along the sofa and held it up to show Molly.

"That *is* a magic brush! Wonderful, thank you! And thank you again for coming today. I really appreciate it."

"We'll see about that," said Constance under her breath.

She did a decent job clearing the evidence of Bobo's misdemeanors, while Molly made the salad dressing and toasted slices of baguette.

"Why oh why did I decide to make profiteroles?" she moaned.

"Because they're yummy?"

"Well, of course, but so are a million other things that don't require a ton of work right before you serve them!"

"They're very high-impact, though, Molls. Just think of what a wow it will be when you walk outside with that platter piled high with them. Are you sticking candles in them? And filling them with ice cream or whipped cream?"

"Ice cream. Sometimes I think I make these ambitious plans just to see if I will tip right over the edge and not come back."

Constance shrugged, not understanding what Molly was going on about.

She made the *pâté à choux* for the profiteroles, grateful that she had picked up a few tips from Nugent during their lesson even while she had been listening intently to his rantings. The bowl barely fit in the small European refrigerator, but she managed to squeeze it in.

The two women continued to work until about two in the afternoon, when Constance went home and Molly lay down to rest. The minute she was stretched out on her bed, thoughts of

Ben and Iris came tumbling into her head, her brain feeling a bit like it was stuffed with a pack of chattering monkeys.

It's not fair for him to be angry with me because Pierre died.

Who pushed you down the stairs, Iris? I don't really believe in any kind of life after death, but what do I know? So if your spirit is listening, give me a sign, will you?

Pierre. Did you get pushed too?

Oh no, I forgot to invite Roger Finsterman!

Molly lurched out of bed and ran her fingers through her hair. Calling Bobo, she headed out through the French doors to the terrace, past the row of tables Eugenia had miraculously scrounged up from somewhere, and walked over to the pigeonnier to invite her other guest, but he was nowhere in evidence.

FRANCES CAME over at around four and found Molly sound asleep in bed.

"Girlfriend, what in the world? You've gotta get ready to par-tay!"

"Oh my heavens," mumbled Molly, rolling over, bleary-eyed. "I didn't mean to fall asleep."

"Well, get into the shower and get with it! Wait 'til you see what you're going to be wearing!" Frances was already dressed for the party in a tight minidress that showed off her long legs. "I found this place in Bordeaux that had almost everything I was looking for! Well, except for shoes. That's always problematic. So we're totally authentic 70s except for the ankles down. I did find one pair of platform boots but they wouldn't have fit any of us."

Molly was staring at Frances, not really following her chatter. Then she blinked hard and shook her head. "Okay! I'm getting in the shower. Did you get anything for Lawrence?"

"Just dropped it off at his place. I'm really glad you're doing this, Molls—he looks so damn sad. Is it still about that guy in Morocco?"

"Not sure," said Molly, putting the bell-bottom pantsuit Frances had given her over the back of a chair and heading to the shower. "But whatever it is, we'll at least show him a lot of love tonight."

❦

MOLLY TRIED to keep her anxiety hidden from her guests and was careful to stick to one kir as she welcomed them at the door. Madame Gervais was the first to arrive.

"I don't have the stamina I used to, you know," she said, in her lilting voice. "But I had a feeling this was a night I didn't want to miss."

"I hope so, Madame Gervais. I very much hope so. What would you like to drink? Thomas, get it for her, please?"

Eugenia was in the kitchen, warming up the camembert-fig tartines, while Molly stood at the door. Bobo was on her best behavior, greeting guests without jumping up on them even once. Into the foyer came Nico and Frances, followed by Roger Finsterman.

"I'm so glad you got my note! How have you been?"

"Terrific burst of productivity, Molly. I'm starting to think La Baraque has magical properties! I've never accomplished so much in so little time, and I'm feeling unusually good about the quality too."

"Wonderful!" said Molly, kissing him on both cheeks and meaning what she said, though it was his optimism she thought was wonderful, not so much his paintings.

More guests piled through the door: Lapin, Caroline Dubois, followed shortly by Tristan Séverin. Angela Langevin, the florist, along with her husband, who looked very studious, wearing a vintage suit and old-fashioned pince-nez. Edmond Nugent arrived, clearly having gotten the message about the party's theme —he was wearing a shirt open to the chest and a pair of tight bell-bottoms that might have been in his closet since 1977.

Thomas handed out lavender spritzers or glasses of Dubonnet to anyone who wanted them, and Constance started the music. Soon the living room was a loud hubbub of villagers drinking and chatting, some moving their hips to Earth, Wind, and Fire and then The Pointer Sisters.

"I don't want you to have to serve," said Molly to Eugenia, who had started making her way through the crowd with a platter of tartines.

"Oh, I don't mind at all. Gives me something to do. It's not like I can talk to anyone!" she said with a wink.

"What I want to know," said Lapin loudly, "is where is the appropriate food? If the theme is 70s American disco, shouldn't we be eating 70s American food?"

"I don't think anyone would want to," said Marie-Claire Lévy with a laugh. "Of course I don't speak from experience. But I did visit America once, and some of the things they ate were positively shocking."

Molly did a quick translation for Eugenia, who had appeared with a fresh tray of tartines.

"Oh now," said Eugenia, smiling at Marie-Claire. "Yes it's true, some things that get popular are too awful for words. Deep-fried Oreos and such-like. But if you ever come visit me in New Orleans, I'll take you to some places that will knock your socks off!"

Marie-Clarie spoke good enough English to follow what Eugenia was saying, but was baffled by what New Orleans food had to do with her socks.

"So what did American eat in the 70s?" asked Lapin.

"Jello?" said Molly. "Space food sticks?"

"Space food sticks?" repeated Lapin wonderingly.

Molly saw Caroline standing alone and excused herself to go

NELL GODDIN

talk to her. "Bonsoir, Caroline!" she said, and kissed cheeks. "I do want to apologize for the other night at Chez Papa. I was unforgivably rude to sit down at your table uninvited."

Caroline gave her a cool look. "Thank you," she said.

"And I know...that this whole thing, all of it, has been terribly hard on you. I'm sorry for that."

"Well, it's hardly your fault, is it? I mean, I see that you like to wedge yourself right in the middle of everything, but honestly, it's got nothing to do with you, has it?"

Molly stood up straight and spoke evenly. "Again, I'm sorry for the difficulties. And despite what you might think, I'm glad you came tonight." She edged past her and went into the kitchen to get a tray of tartines to pass around. Then she heard Ben's voice, and a stab of some feeling she couldn't identify went through her. It had been days since they'd seen each other, or even spoken.

I'm not running over to him, she thought defiantly. Not after how snippy he was to me the other day. He can come to me.

Almost everyone who was invited was there—she had figured Lawrence would wait a bit so he could make an entrance, but where was he? She stood on tip-toes to check out the crowd, and the guests looked happy and ready for a good time. The room had gotten loud and it was time to invite them out to the grassy dance floor and get them moving.

And then? Well, she didn't quite know. She was pretty sure she had the dynamite *and* the match, but how to get one thing close enough to the other for the desired explosion to occur?

37

Molly was dancing the Bus Stop with a kir in one hand when she heard shrieking from inside the house. It sounded like shrieks of hilarity but she was on edge and ran inside with trepidation. There in the living room, finally, stood the guest of honor—Lawrence, in his glory, posing in a white bell-bottomed suit, shirt open with a gold chain twinkling on his chest.

Everyone in the room was howling, which noise only got rowdier when the first notes of "The Love Machine" started playing and Lawrence's hips started to twitch. He reached for Molly's hand and the two of them whirled through a number of disco moves including the Bump, the Butterfly, and even the Point Move. When the song was over she fell into his arms and they roared with laughter.

"Not bad, Molly," he said, taking out a handkerchief and mopping his brow. "I had no idea there was a disco queen lurking inside you."

Molly went to the bar Thomas had set up on the kitchen counter and poured herself a lavender spritzer. "Well, you know, disco was something my girlfriends and I used to do together when we were around twelve, that age right between childhood and being teenagers. We were very serious about getting all the moves just right," she added with a laugh. "We studied Saturday Night Fever like a sacred text."

"Drink, birthday boy?" asked Nico, already starting a Negroni.

Lawrence nodded, smiling. "I must say, Frances out-did herself. Can you believe she found this outfit? And in my size? She is a miracle worker."

Nico smiled dreamily.

"She's outside teaching line dancing to everyone. You know, if I ever get married again—which, shut up, I don't expect to, I'm just ruminating here—the guy has *got* to be able to dance. That was just too much fun."

"Oh, so you're going to marry a gay man then?"

Molly laughed.

"I resent that," said Nico, handing Lawrence his Negroni.

"So do I," said Caroline, who appeared next to Molly with her eyebrows furrowed.

"He's joking. Joking!" said Molly. "Though just as a data point, I've never had a boyfriend who could dance. Or who knows, maybe they could have. They were unwilling to try."

"I seem to remember Ben acquitting himself quite handsomely on the dance floor at the Gala last year," said Lawrence with raised eyebrows.

Molly shrugged. There was an uncomfortable silence. She craned her neck to see if she could see Ben somewhere, but did not. He was probably outside with the crowd. Maybe he was dancing.

I've been so unforgiving. I'm a terrible girlfriend.

"Lawrence, you made such a fashionably late entrance that you missed all the tartines, and let me tell you, they were absolutely fantastic!" said Molly.

"Concur," said Nico, smiling. "But you're changing the subject."

Molly waved him off.

"I'll make up for missing the tartines with unrestrained gluttony for all the remaining courses," answered Lawrence. "Now I must go greet my public." And he swanned out through the French doors to the terrace, leaving the rest of them still giggling over his outfit.

Molly consulted with Eugenia about whether it was time to serve the duck, and then followed Lawrence outside. She was keeping an eye on several guests, wanting to monitor their demeanor and whom they were talking to. Nugent was sitting by himself at the long table, glowering at the dancers in the yard. Caroline had followed her outside and was standing with her arms crossed, also glowering.

The rest of the guests were were living it up—dancing, drinking, and eating the last crumbs of hors d'oeuvres. She even saw Madame Gervais on the dance floor, waggling her hands in the air and supported by the ever-gentlemanly Rémy. Tristan Séverin had not brought his wife and was dancing with Marie-Claire Lévy, his arms and legs flying out all over everywhere, looking as though he was having the time of his life.

To her surprise, Molly had a pang of missing Pierre. It was easy to imagine him there, looking uncomfortable in that gruff way he had, but showing up nonetheless. After hearing of his death, she had tried out the idea that he had murdered his wife and then killed himself out of guilt, but the idea hadn't stuck with her, and after much thought she had realized a few things that put him entirely in the clear. At least—*if* she was right.

She knew she had to make peace with Ben. He had been right all along about Pierre, and the least she could do was admit that. But the guests needed to be served their duck and ratatouille, and the profiteroles had to be stuffed with ice cream. First things first.

❦

ONCE EVERYONE WAS SEATED at the long table—which was covered with a simple white tablecloth and bowls of roses from Molly's garden—Eugenia, Nico, and Molly came around with big platters of duck confit and served. Thomas followed with a platter of ratatouille, and the salad was held for a separate course the way the French do it.

Cheryl Lynn's "Got To Be Real" was playing, and the glitter ball twinkled as it hung from a nearby oak. Constance turned down the music to make conversation easier; one heard French, English, and much laughter and joking as the guests dug into the feast and filled their glasses. A casual observer might have thought the party was the picture of village cheer, a group of friends enjoying a birthday celebration on a warm summer night.

But perhaps a more alert observer would have noticed that not everyone at the table was feeling joyful, or even sociable.

Molly took a seat next to Caroline and across from Nugent and Séverin. Ben was sitting at the far end with Maron and Monsour, who were watching the guests with something of the detachment that scientists might show as they observe pond creatures under a microscope.

After pointing at the gendarmes discreetly, Caroline asked, "Do you think they are, um, *on duty* even here at a party?" She was sitting next to Nathalie Marchand, the manager of the almost-Michelin-rated restaurant, La Métairie.

"Might be," whispered Nathalie. "You must have heard—we had a murder take place right in the restaurant last year! I met Gilles Maron during all of that. He's...he's actually rather nice, though he doesn't make the best first impression."

"I'll say," said Caroline. "I don't like gendarmes, police, any of it."

"Have some wine?" asked Nathalie, picking up the jug of red.

Across from Molly, Nugent picked at his duck.

"Don't tell me you only eat sweets!" Molly teased.

Glumly, he lifted his eyes from his plate, then made a theatrical shrug.

Next to him, Tristan was chatting to Marie-Claire, who sat on his other side, about his plan to take the ten year-olds on a rock-climbing trip the following spring. Marie-Claire was a good listener and seemed interested in Severin's scheme, interrupting with a question every so often as Severin's enthusiasm bubbled along.

Okay. It's showtime.

"Tristan, that does sound like an adventure they'll never forget," Molly said, joining in to their conversation. Nugent shot her a dark look.

"Oh, the young ones love trying something new like that!" he answered. "Their heads are so full of fantasy, you know. They'll imagine themselves as heros, scaling heights to save the princess!"

Molly took a quick breath. "Speaking of princesses, I know you and everyone here who knew Iris must be thinking about her tonight. I was wondering—do you think it would be all right to make a toast to her, or some sort of remembrance?"

Nugent narrowed his eyes at her. Séverin bowed his head for a moment and then looked at Molly with a sad smile.

"Oh yes, of course, all of us are thinking of her. Iris...an amazing woman. Everyone would say so." He raised his glass, the disco light catching the wetness in his eyes.

"Well...I don't mean to get overly personal, but you know how crass Americans are sometimes," Molly said with a laugh that anyone who knew her well would know was utterly fake. "And nosy, too. So I was wondering...did something happen to change your mind about her? I mean, word has gotten out about the email you sent. The night she died, actually, now that I think of it."

Séverin looked at Molly with surprise. "What?"

"Oh come on, you know what I'm talking about. What I heard was—you *broke up with her* by email. Isn't that sort of bad etiquette, Tristan? I mean, not to get all schoolmarmish on you, but surely that's something people ought to do in person?"

Séverin's eyes opened wide. Molly imagined she could hear the whirring of his brain working. He was still for a long moment, then expelled a bark of a laugh as he looked both ways down the long table as though to see if anyone else was listening. He leaned forward and said in a low voice, "The truth is, Molly, I had gotten to the point...I was focused on trying to do right by my dear wife. I hate to say it...but you see, I tried to break it off with Iris several times before that—in person as you say—but she was very persistent. In the end, it seemed the only way to shake her."

Nugent had leaned in so as not to miss what Séverin was saying. After a momentary pause he leapt to his feet and exploded, "*Shake* her? What kind of *merde* are you spouting, you sickening excuse for a man!"

The table went quiet. Thomas hurried over to Molly's laptop and turned off the music.

"I cannot imagine how you managed to pull the wool over her eyes in the first place!" Nugent continued. "But I will *never* believe that she was clinging to you and wouldn't let go. Never!"

Séverin patted Nugent on the shoulder, which he could do without standing up because he was so much taller than Nugent. "Settle down, my friend. It's all over now, right? We're here to celebrate Mr. Weebly's birthday!" He raised his glass and then took a gulp, but no one followed suit. All down the table, people were staring and paying close attention to the drama unfolding.

Molly watched Nugent, praying he would not go silent, not now.

Nugent pulled away from Séverin's touch with an expression of disgust. He walked up towards the end of the table where Ben, Maron, and Monsour sat, all eyes on him.

"All right then, if it's come to this...I absolutely must speak, no matter how personally embarrasing it might be. I am sorry for not doing so sooner." He looked soberly at the gendarmes. "*I* wrote that email, not Séverin!" he said loudly, his voice quavering.

"What is he saying?" Caroline asked Nathalie. Molly got up and followed Nugent to the end of the table.

"Go on," Ben said to him calmly.

"I don't think there is one person here who would say that Tristan Séverin deserved to wipe Iris Gault's feet!" Nugent continued. "I couldn't believe it when I heard they were..." He shook his head as though to cast out the distasteful image of the couple. "I had hoped it was nothing but gossip. But then I saw the *poem*," he spat.

"What poem is he talking about?" Caroline said to Nathalie, who had no idea what was going on, being way behind in village gossip.

Nugent looked down the table at the guests and sneered,"Oh, so you're all thinking how lovely, how romantic, the school principal wrote the beautiful Iris a poem. Well, I'll tell you, it was nothing but filth. To the village goddess—filth! She deserved so much better. Someone who understood her...someone...."

"Someone...like you?" said Monsour, eliciting some nervous chuckles.

Nugent shook his head. He reached down and absently took a long pull from Monsour's glass of wine and then rubbed his forehead with his fingers, something Molly had seen him do when he became agitated.

"The poem was in Severin's desk, in the school office. That's where you saw it? What were you doing there?" asked Ben.

Maron kicked himself for not thinking of the question himself.

Nugent tried to wave Dufort off, and go back to his seat. His shoulders drooped and his face sagged, as though he were suddenly twenty years older.

But Maron stood up and held his arm. "No, Monsieur, I believe you have some questions to answer."

"Shall I get handcuffs?" asked Monsour brightly.

"Not necessary," said Maron. "Answer the question, please. The poem was in the school office. Is that where you saw it?"

Nugent nodded, staring at the ground.

"And this was when you also gained access to Séverin's computer?" asked Ben, unable to stay quiet now that he saw what must have happened. Nugent did not respond, so he continued, "It was you who sent the email breaking up with Iris, not Séverin? That is what you are admitting?"

Molly was barely able to contain her impatience when Nugent did not answer right away. "Well?" she said, and then clamped her mouth shut and told herself to let the thing play out without interfering.

"So what if I did!" Nugent blurted out finally. "The idea of him with her—it was unbearable to me! He is nothing but a light-weight, a mere child, what right did he have—"

"It is interesting to me that you think you get to decide who does what, who deserves what," said Maron. "Perhaps you believe it is also your job to decide who has a right to live and who does not?"

Monsour stood on Nugent's other side, clamping his hand on his arm, and waited for Maron's instructions.

Wait, what?

This was not the direction Molly was expecting things to take. But it was out of her hands now. She had lit the match and could not control who got hurt in the explosion.

38

Ben was on his feet. "When were you in the school office?" he asked Nugent. "Think carefully, Edmond. What night was it?"

"The night she was killed!" said Caroline, jumping up from the table and knocking over her wine. "It was *you* I saw in the office that night night, wasn't it? Not Tristan!" She turned to face her boss, who leaned back in his chair and smiled.

"Oh, take your seat, Caroline!" he said. "Don't get involved in this—it's just silly drama. You know how Nugent is."

"You mean, in love with Iris? Yes, I do know. I know exactly how that is." Caroline was backing away from Séverin, just as Dufort was coming towards him. The other guests were looking from one end of the table to other, not quite understanding, and not wanting to miss anything. No one moved, not even to take a sip of wine.

"Please refresh our memories, Caroline," Dufort said. "Can you describe what you saw, the night Iris died?"

"Murdered," said Caroline. "Don't say 'died' when you mean 'murdered'. All right." Caroline did not take her eyes off Séverin as she reached for Nathalie's wine-glass and took a gulp from it. "I went for a walk. It was a hot night and I was feeling restless. My apartment is not far from the school and I happened to go down that street. I noticed Séverin's car parked outside which I thought was a little strange."

"Strange?"

"Yes. It was after dark. He is not known for being a workaholic, let's just put it that way," she said bitterly. "Though in my defense, I figured he was rushing to finish up some work that should have been done weeks ago."

"So his car was parked where?"

"In the small area reserved for the school. So when I saw someone in the office—it was dark, the lights weren't even turned on, all I could see was sort of a silhouette, or just a shape, really, from the glow of a computer screen—I just assumed...."

Molly couldn't help it, she grinned.

"...I just assumed it was Séverin, sitting at his desk. Finally getting around to doing some of the work I'd been after him to get done."

Dufort turned back to Nugent. "But it was not Séverin at all, was it?"

Maron came up behind Dufort and stood on the other side of Séverin.

"Oh, of course it was me!" Séverin jumped in to say. "My car was there, right?"

"Why did you go to the school office?" Maron asked Nugent. "This is not the testimony you gave when I interviewed you."

"No, no, of course it isn't! And *mon Dieu* it's not the testimony I want to give now! I would like everything to go backwards, backwards to the day when Iris was still alive, and see if any of us fools could do something to stop what happened." He put his face in his hands. "All I wanted...all I wanted was for her to be happy...."

"I don't *believe* you," said Caroline to Séverin, her voice rising. "At least—all this time, I thought at least you *cared* about her. Even if you were being a total jerk, I thought she really mattered to you. I never, ever dreamed you'd be the one...."

Séverin stood up slowly. "I don't appreciate these insinuations," he said, holding his palms up. He took a step backwards but Maron was on one side and Monsour the other.

"I'm afraid your alibi has just collapsed," Maron said.

"You went to the Gault's that night," Molly said to Séverin. "Left your car at the school and walked over. It was Iris who wanted to break up with you, wasn't it?"

Séverin attempted to chuckle. "Oh, you know, that was...she didn't mean anything by it. God love her but Iris could be flighty, you know what I'm saying?"

"*Flighty?*" said Nugent, rushing up and shoving the taller man in the chest. Monsour pulled Nugent back and held him. At this point the guests at the table could stay quiet no longer and a loud murmur sprang up. Lawrence could be heard saying he had never had a birthday party quite like this one.

"You went over to the Gault's," Molly repeated. "Had tea, I believe? You left your teacup in the living room. It stood out, you see, because the Gaults were so tidy. And then you tried to convince Iris not to leave you, isn't that right? And perhaps... perhaps you didn't mean to, but as you fought, the two of you got closer to the stairs, and...."

Séverin looked around, searching for an ally, but found no one. He started to speak. He sat back down and then stood up again. He looked at Molly, Nugent, Dufort, and the two gendarmes, smoothing his palm over his cheek. Finally he hung his head and murmured, "I just couldn't stand her leaving, you understand? I'm not some cold blooded killer. I loved her. I really, really loved her."

As Maron and Monsour led him away, Lawrence noted aloud

the irony of that statement, and the guests murmured their agreement.

Feeling triumphant but also sad, Molly turned to look for Ben, but he was headed around the side of the house, the glitter-ball throwing colored dots on his back as he walked away.

🕸 39 🕸

It was a sort of tradition, after a killer had been caught, for Molly and her friends to have a celebration at Chez Papa and talk over the the details of what happened. Not this time. Molly and Ben had still not spoken. When Molly talked to Lawrence the next day, he said all he wanted to do was come to La Baraque to eat leftovers just with Molly, and that is what they did.

"I just got some news," Molly said when Lawrence came inside. "The toxicology report came back on Pierre. Narcotics. Not enough to overdose, but still, apparently a pretty big dose."

"Enough to make him lose his balance."

"Exactly."

"Well, at least he wasn't murdered. I guess that's something. Did Ben tell you?"

"I guess Nagrand had lunch at Chez Papa today, and Nico called to pass it on." She sighed. "Sorry, the salad is a little wilted," she said, handing him a plate. "Do you want to eat on the terrace?"

"Yes. But first I'm putting my slippers on. I love that we're having a sleep-over, just like we did after the Amy Bennett case."

"Okay, put on your slippers and grab the wine, will you?" Molly went out, Bobo at her heels.

"I have a lot of questions," said Lawrence. "Shall I begin with the ones about how in the world you figured out Séverin pushed poor Iris down the stairs? Or I have some more personal questions if you'd rather I start with those." He raised his eyebrows at her and poured them some wine.

"If it's about Ben, I honestly have nothing to tell you. I don't know what's going on. Only we're not talking, which obviously isn't a good sign."

Lawrence looked at his friend to gauge her feelings, then sliced off a hunk of duck confit and ate it. "No, I suppose not," he said finally. "But maybe a bit of a break from each other will be... clarifying? I'm really in no position to give advice on romantic matters. All right, let's leave that subject for the moment. Now tell me: how did you start to suspect Séverin? Everyone loved him, or so I thought. The last thing I'd ever have imagined is that he's a cold-blooded killer."

"I know. To be a little fair, we don't know his intentions when he went to see Iris that night. Maybe he was only trying to talk her into staying with him and at some point he lost control. But you're right, he doesn't fit any of our ideas about murderers, does he? And that fact almost let him get away with it. That, plus a lot of luck. It's not like he planned for Nugent to break into his office while he was with Iris that night—that was pure chance, and gave him what appeared to be a rock-solid alibi when Caroline thought she saw him there."

"So how did you guess it wasn't Séverin after all?"

"Well, nobody was making any progress with case. Not me, Ben, or the gendarmes. I figured we'd overlooked something important—or not overlooked exactly—that we'd assumed something incorrectly, or taken something for granted. That we thought we knew something when we actually didn't. Anyway, I went back through every detail that we had so far, trying to look at it completely objectively. Holding the facts of the case up in the light and looking at them upside down and backwards...." Molly took a sip of wine. "And that didn't get me anywhere either. But it did sort of prepare my brain, if you know what I mean?"

"Sort of?"

"I mean that when the break came, I was ready to notice it. I was having a pastry lesson with Nugent. The poor man was obsessed with Iris, so much so that for a little while I thought maybe *he* had totally lost his grip and killed her, in a moment of total insanity or something. But anyway, the other day I was in his shop and he was showing me how to make *pâté à choux*, which is how I learned to make your profiteroles last night." She stopped to eat some salad, slowly wiping her mouth with her napkin as she remembered the afternoon with Nugent.

"Come on, Molly, stop dragging it out!"

"All right, have some patience," she laughed. "So...he's ranting away about Séverin, utterly furious and jealous that Iris had an affair with him instead of with Nugent. He started saying how Séverin had broken up with her, had just tossed her aside when he got tired of her, that's the kind of horrible man he was. He wanted me to agree that Séverin hadn't deserved her."

Lawrence cocked his head, not getting it.

"Don't you see? Nobody knew about the supposed break-up except for the gendarmes, plus Ben and me. The only reason any of us knew about it is that Maron had taken Severin's computer and found the email on his hard drive, along with a folder of emails the couple had written to each other over the course of the affair. In other words, the only source for the breakup was that one email—no village gossip, letters, witnesses, nothing else at all.

"Nugent had no way to know anything about it," she continued, "...unless he had written it himself."

"And since it was sent from Séverin's computer, you knew Nugent must've broken in there to send it."

"Exactly. And then it was no great leap to realize that the man

Caroline saw in the school office that night was not Séverin, but Nugent. She assumed it was her boss because, well, it was the school office. The man was sitting at Séverin's desk, at Séverin's computer. She worked with him there everyday. His car was parked right outside. There was no reason for her to question it because Caroline had no idea someone else had a motive for being there. And she said it was typical for Séverin to let things at work slide and then have to scramble to get stuff done in time."

"It must have made Nugent furious that he ended up inadvertently giving Séverin an alibi."

"I think it did," Molly said. "He was certainly terribly unhappy, and agitated. For a moment there, when the affair was discovered, we had the right idea—that Séverin might have killed Iris in a jealous rage because she had ended the affair—but once it appeared he had broken up with her *and* he had an alibi…well, we totally crossed him off the lists of suspects."

"Who were you looking at then?"

Molly considered. "My backup choice was Nugent. But I was fairly convinced it was Pierre almost up until he died."

They were silent for a while, taking a moment to appreciate the magnificent leftovers and the starry night. "One thing that's bothering me. I think that I let some emotions that had absolutely nothing to do with the case get in the way of my thinking. When Ben got mad at me for wanting to consider Pierre guilty, I got all competitive about it. I was insisting it was Pierre because I wanted Ben to be wrong and me to be right. It was stupid. And I can't help feeling guilty, because what if we'd caught Séverin much sooner? Would Pierre not have…?"

"I see what you're saying. But I think the point is, you did figure it out in the end. And Pierre's taking those pills had nothing to do with Séverin, at least not about his being caught or not caught. He did it because he was in so much pain from losing Iris."

Molly nodded, not entirely convinced. "Pierre was an odd

duck," she said finally. "I have a lot of questions I'd like to ask him. Like—that teacup. When I went to the Gault house after Iris was murdered, I noticed it right away, sitting on a table in the living room. The Gaults were fastidious people and that empty cup stood out like a flashing red light. Now, why did Pierre leave it there?"

"I wonder if he knew who left it. And wanted you to see it."

Molly's eyes widened. "But in that case, why not just point it out? For sure it would have had Séverin's DNA on it."

Now it was Lawrence's turn to shrug. "More likely he was simply so undone about his wife's murder that he wasn't tidying up like he usually did. I have the feeling he loved Iris more than anyone gave him credit for. Maybe including Iris herself."

"Maybe. But then why did he say he called the ambulance, when the emergency number has no record of the call?"

"Imagine, Molly. Imagine what it would be like to live through your beloved spouse having an affair. Your heart is breaking. You stay late at work because it's so painful to see her brighten up when she leaves to go meet him. And one day you come home to find her lying at the foot of the stairs, crumpled up, dead. The absolute love of your life."

"I have had some experience with a cheating spouse," she said quietly.

"Tell me if I'm wrong, but I've never had the idea from you that Donnie was your passion, your deepest love. Am I mistaken?"

"...No. You're not."

"Well, I'll just say...that from my experience in Morocco, with Julio...I can understand how a trauma like what Pierre experienced...might make him behave in unexpected ways. Maybe he thought he did call. Maybe he knew right away it was no use. Maybe he hardly even knew what he was saying."

Molly nodded.

"One thing about Pierre—he held everything in. It shouldn't

be a surprise that when tragedy struck, his natural inclination for stoicism got even stronger. Anyway. Besides Pierre, any other suspects?"

"Ah," said Molly. "Let me bring out dessert for that conversation. I need to fill a few profiterole shells with ice cream and heat up the chocolate sauce, I'll be right back."

"That sounds heavenly. Hurry!"

❧

LAWRENCE GOT up and wandered into the meadow while he waited for Molly and dessert. He saw the orange cat prowling through the tall grass, and lights on in the pigeonnier. Then he thought about his Moroccan friend Julio, and his crooked smile, and ran his hand over his eyes with a sigh.

"Okay, tell me," said Lawrence a few minutes later, scraping several profiteroles onto his dessert plate as soon as Molly had put down the platter. "Oh my heavenly Father, these look good. Last night got so crazy I don't even remember eating any."

"Well, you did. A substantial pile, if I remember correctly, which I do."

Lawrence laughed and sighed again as he chewed, more happily this time. "So...other suspects? You wouldn't tell me a thing during the investigation, so now I want all the details."

Molly finished her first profiterole and helped herself to several more. "Ben was thinking Caroline Dubois."

Lawrence looked up sharply. "I've known Caro for years," he said. "She's quite unhappy. But a murderer?"

"It took a while for me to unravel what was going on there. Things weren't adding up, you know? When I first met her, she lied about Séverin's having an affair with Iris. I didn't understand why she would do that, especially once she admitted she too had a crush on Iris. I'll tell you, the more people I talked to, the sorrier

I was that I never got to know her. She had most of the village under her spell!"

"Not me," said Lawrence, with a twinkle in his eye.

"Oh, really? Female beauty really does nothing at all for you?"

"I appreciate yours," said Lawrence, grinning. "And hers too. It's just that...I could see that some of the reason so many people went ga-ga over her was that Iris...all right, she was very beautiful, and also she kept herself held in. You never for one minute got the feeling that she was letting out what she actually thought or felt about much of anything."

Molly nodded. "It's sad to think that she never really got to embrace her life. At least that's how it looks from the outside. She was so restrained, so controlled."

"Very. And so, in my opinion, people were then free to imagine all sorts of things about her. They could make her into anything they wanted, because she presented something of a blank slate."

"Huh. Interesting idea. But Séverin and Dubois—they knew Iris better than that. They worked with her for years."

"And maybe the affair was the one time she finally let her hair down. Understandable that Caro would have a difficult time. I mean, think about it: she's in love with a straight woman, so the whole thing is doomed from the get-go. And then her boss zips in and steals her, right from under her nose, and she has to see them together day after day."

"That's gotta hurt."

"Yeah. Plus Séverin treated her badly. Caroline had written Iris a poem, laying all her feelings out there—and Séverin found it. And he sent it to Iris without a word that he hadn't actually written it himself."

"Quite a betrayal. And incidentally, how did you find that out?"

"I get to keep a few secrets, Lawrence. Or...I'll tell you if you share your sources?"

"Never in this life, my dear. Isn't this the most exquisite night? I could lean back and look at the stars for hours if it didn't start to make me crabby about not having anyone to share it with."

"Excuse me?"

"You know perfectly well what I mean." He reached his arm around his friend and the two of them finished the bottle of wine and kept looking up into the sky, filled with the usual swirling and conflicting emotions that is the human condition. Ben was off somewhere, doing something, as was Julio. Frances and Nico were presumably blissfully planning their wedding.

But Molly and Lawrence were happy too, if a different kind of happy, and there was no point in wishing for a different flavor. Peace and calm reigned again in Castillac, and there were enough leftovers in the refrigerator for at least two more meals.

And importantly, the proprietor of the best pâtisserie in the village had not been guilty of murder after all. That alone was something to celebrate.

THE END

ALSO BY NELL GODDIN

GLOSSARY

Chapter 1
    fêtes.......celebration
    salut........hey, hi
    bonsoir....good evening
    pâté.........delicious paste made of ground meat, fat, and spices
    La Baraque...house, shack. Name of Molly's house (and gîte business)

Chapter 2
    cantine........school cafeteria
    gîtes...........holiday rentals
    pigeonnier......place to house pigeons; dovecote

Chapter 3
    pâtisserie........pastry shop

Chapter 4:
    mousse au chocolat....chocolate mousse

Chapter 5

en vacances.....on vacation

coucou.............hey there, hello (said to get someone's attention)

Chapter 6

Excusez-moi! Il y a quelqu'un....Excuse me! Is anybody there?

bon sang...........exclamation of frustration, such as 'for heaven's sake'. Literally, good blood.

Chapter 10

bon...........good

Merci, à bientôt......thanks, see you soon

Chapter 11

oui.........yes

département....French version of county

Chapter 19

tutoyer.......unlike English, French has both a formal and a familiar way of addressing someone. Using the 'tu' form of 'you' is familiar, what you would use with family and friends.

Chapter 20

chérie..............dear

mairie...........town hall

Chapter 21

colombages.........half-timbered

Chapter 24

merde.......impolite word for excrement

Chapter 26

coup de foudre......thunderbolt

Chapter 30
à tous...................to everyone

Chapter 33
Jésuits..................flaky pastry filled with almond cream
palmiers...............pastry, supposedly shaped like a palm-leaf
pâtissier..............pastry chef
tart tatin.............buttery apple tart

Chapter 35
duxelles................small dumplings
lardons...................bacon
ratatouille...........a stewed dish of tomatoes, eggplant, onions, zucchini, and garlic
confit..................a preparation that involves submerging meat in fat, which preserves it. Makes the meat very succulent.
profiteroles........a great pile of cream puffs drizzled with chocolate sauce

Chapter 36
pâté à choux.................cream puff paste

Chapter 38
mon Dieu.................my God

ACKNOWLEDGMENTS

Enormous thanks to Nancy Kelley for saving the day, and to Tommy Glass and Heather Penner for their sharp eyes.

Also a grateful shout-out to the best readers a writer could have, who give me terrific feedback and catch the billions of typos.

ABOUT THE AUTHOR

Nell Goddin lives in Virginia but dreams of living in France again someday. Hopefully by then the dogs will have calmed down enough that the neighbors won't want her to move away.

www.nellgoddin.com
nell@nellgoddin.com

Made in the USA
Middletown, DE
04 May 2022

65281983R00156